FLY AWAY

**Center Point
Large Print**

FLY AWAY

Lynn N. Austin

Center Point Publishing
Thorndike, Maine

This Center Point Large Print edition is published in the year 2006 by arrangement with the author.

Copyright © 1996 by Lynn N. Austin.

The text of this Large Print edition is unabridged. In other aspects, this book may vary from the original edition. Printed in Thailand. Set in 16-point Times New Roman type.

ISBN 1-58547-719-2

Library of Congress Cataloging-in-Publication Data

Austin, Lynn N.
 Fly away / Lynn N. Austin.--Center Point large print ed.
  p. cm.
 ISBN 1-58547-719-2 (lib. bdg. : alk. paper)
  1. Large type books. I. Title.

PS3551.U839F59 2006
813'.54--dc22

2005022920

Dedicated to Bonnie Auer and Peggy Hach.
I'm proud to call you my sisters,
blessed to call you my friends.

My heart is in anguish within me;
the terrors of death assail me . . .

. . . "Oh, that I had wings like a dove!
I would fly away and be at rest—"
Ps. 55:4, 6

1

Wednesday, September 2, 1987

Mike Dolan sat alone in the tiny examining room, kneading a baseball cap in his sweating hands. Any minute now the doctor would enter.

He shifted in his seat, wishing he could move around and walk off some of his anxiety, but the room was too cramped. He had flown in cockpits that were bigger. He'd already studied all the diplomas on the office walls, but they hadn't distracted him from his fears for very long. He could scarcely make heads or tails of them, with their fancy foreign words and swirly script.

He stood up, kicked off his work boots, then stepped onto the doctor's scale, fiddling with the shiny weights, sliding them back and forth until they balanced. One hundred and sixty-three pounds. Not good. He had lost more weight. He considered playing with the sliding height bar, but he already knew what that would tell him. He stood exactly five feet, five and three-quarter inches in his stocking feet. Forty-some years ago his muscular build had turned a lot of gals' heads, especially when he wore his U.S. Air Force pilot's uniform. He glanced in the mirror over the tiny sink and smoothed down his receding ring of white hair. Every Christmas his grandkids tried to convince him to pad his belly, grow a white beard, and play Santa Claus down at the mall. "You'd be perfect, Grandpa," they insisted. He studied his reflection, stroking his smooth chin. Resembling Santa Claus wasn't all that bad. Mike sat down again with a weary groan and bent to retie his shoes.

He looked at his watch. Ever since the nurse had parked him in this windowless cell 12 minutes ago he had been forced to listen to a piano playing classical music somewhere in the distance. Now it was starting to get on his nerves. Mike was no musician, but even he could tell that the blasted thing was out of tune. It seemed like a bad omen.

Piano music in a medical complex? Where could the sound be coming from? It didn't tinkle from a speaker like the usual canned office music but drifted, soft and muffled, and seemed to come from behind the thin wall of the room next door. Mike pondered the mystery for a while before remembering that the Cancer Center had offices and a lounge for outpatients in this building. He thought he remembered seeing a big black piano in the lounge when he visited the center after his first cancer surgery a few years ago. That must be it.

With the mystery solved, once again Mike had nothing to do. He leaned forward to study the wife-and-family snapshots on the doctor's desk, while the piano hammered away like a hailstorm on a hangar roof. He didn't care much for that fancy, highbrow music. Made him restless.

The doctor's outer waiting room had been crowded with people, and Mike wondered how many of them had come for their test results as he had. It occurred to him that this little drama must take place dozens of times a day in offices like this one, all over the country, maybe all over the world. Some folks got good news and went home to their families breathing easy and smiling again. Others got bad news. He wondered how most people handled that kind of news. He'd had plenty of time to think about it in the week or so since taking this tests. Mike Dolan knew exactly what he was going to do.

Now it sounded as if the pianist next door was trying to do loops and dives and barrel rolls on a keyboard. As soon as his appointment ended, no matter what the outcome, Mike decided he would drive back to the airport and take one of his planes up for a few loops and dives and barrel rolls of his own. He shifted impatiently in the chair, anxious to grab some sky.

Finally he heard footsteps and Dr. Bennett's mumbling voice outside in the hallway. He perched his cap on his head for a moment and wiped his palms on his thighs. He couldn't greet the doctor with a clammy handshake. Mike could picture the doctor removing his chart from the plastic holder on the door and studying it: MICHAEL G. DOLAN, MALE CAUCASIAN, AGE 65, CANCER: COLON [C2] Right Hemicolectomy 1984, suspected recurrence.

Mike waited, unconsciously holding his breath. He

remembered the last time; the ugly helplessness of lying flat on his back in the hospital, the pitying looks everyone gave him, their forced smiles and the hushed tone of their voices. No matter what, he wouldn't go through that again. Nor would he get fogged in with a lot of self-pity if the cancer had returned. He had lived a long, happy life, full of fun and adventure, and if this was the end for him, well, he shouldn't complain. He didn't know much about the hereafter, but he figured it would probably be the greatest flight of his life— like flying without the plane.

Next door, the music soared in altitude to the top of the scale, then crashed with a resounding finale. Mike shook his head. That piano made for a pretty rough landing.

Finally the door opened and Dr. Bennett entered with a folder. The doctor was in his 50s, tall and angular, with unruly black hair and dark circles under his eyes. His grim expression made Mike's heart race. They shook hands.

"How are you, Mike?"

"Well, I guess you should know."

"Pardon?"

"Fine, Doc. I'm fine." Why did people always say *fine* whether they were or not?

The doctor's chair squeaked as he dropped into it. He took his time studying the test results, tapping his bony fingers on the desk, pursing his lips. He looked down at the papers, not meeting Mike's eyes. A bad sign.

"Mike, according to these lab reports it appears there are liver metastases."

Mike felt his stomach flop over, as if he'd suddenly hit an updraft. "What does that mean?"

"It means the cancer has spread to your liver."

"Are you sure?"

"I'm afraid so."

Mike thought he'd prepared himself for this, but suddenly a surge of panic rushed through him, the same gut-twisting fear a novice pilot feels when his engine suddenly cuts out on him during flight. If Mike was sitting in a cockpit he'd know from years of experience what to do. But he wasn't in a cockpit now. He was in uncharted territory. And he was flying blind. A surge of emotions pulled him steadily down against his will, and he fought with the desperate instincts of a pilot in a fatal flat spin to regain control. As if on cue, the piano next door began to play a slow, sad song in sympathy, just like in the movies.

"I'd like to schedule you for some tests to determine if you're a candidate for resection," Dr. Bennett continued. Mike barely heard him. It wasn't true. They'd made a mistake. His thoughts whirled dizzily, out of control.

Suddenly he thought of Helen, and the memory of his wife's courage as she'd faced death, unexpectedly quieted his racing heart. He was in command again, his emotions responding to his control, his will determining his course. With a faint smile and a barely perceptible nod, he affirmed his calm acceptance of the truth. *Don't play any sad songs for me,* he wanted to tell the pianist. *Let me go out with a jig.*

". . . And if the tests show you are a candidate for resection, I'd like to schedule you for further surgery," Dr. Bennett said.

"Hold on, Doc. What's the bottom line here? I'm probably going to die anyway, right?" He smiled, hoping it would assure the doctor that he could handle the truth. Dr. Bennett closed the file and folded his hands on top of it.

"The cancer has spread. There's probably no way to stop it or remove all the malignant cells."

"Then why operate again?"

"The longevity rate is about 15 percent in successful candidates for resection and—"

"No. If it's just a matter of time, I'd rather not prolong it." Mike had thought through this scene, and he recited his lines in response to the doctor's cues like a well-rehearsed play.

"Well, in some cases, surgery and chemotherapy can offer patients a little more time. Make them more comfortable—"

"That stuff's not for me."

"Listen, Mike—"

"There's really no point, you know what I mean? If surgery can't cure me, then why bother with it? I don't want to go back in the hospital and put my family through that mess again."

"Well, just let me outline the course of treatment I would like to advise."

Mike smiled. "No thanks. Just tell me how long I've got."

The doctor picked up a thin, gold pen from his desk and began to toy with it. "It's hard to say for sure."

"Take an educated guess. I won't sue you if you're wrong."

Dr. Bennett looked away. "Unless you consent to surgery and chemotherapy . . . maybe three months. Six at the most."

Mike repeated the words to himself but he barely comprehended them. He had three months to live. Six at the most.

In the room next door the piano wrung out sympathy like a cleaning lady wrings out a floor mop, but the out-of-tune notes made it sound as comical as an old silent movie. Mike imagined all the blue-haired ladies who volunteered at the Cancer Center reaching for their hankies. He smiled to himself.

"Thanks, Doc. I appreciate you giving it to me straight."

Now that Mike knew the truth, he wanted to get as far away from this tiny office as he could and get on with what remained of his life. Smell the fall air. Soar the blue skies. He stood and edged toward the door. The doctor's chair groaned as he swiveled to face him.

"Please think about it some more, Mike. Talk it over with your family, at least. And if you change your mind, I can fit you in the schedule right away." Mike nodded vaguely and opened the door. "May I give the

Cancer Center your name?" the doctor asked. "They provide a lot of helpful services."

"Sure. Whatever." Halfway out the door Mike paused and turned back. "By the way, how often do they play that awful piano next door?" He motioned toward the wall with his thumb.

"You mean at the Cancer Center? I don't know . . . maybe once or twice a month. Mostly for fundraisers and social events, I guess."

"Then I'd buy some earplugs if I were you. See you later, Doc."

He waved his cap in salute, then pulled it over his bald spot and strolled through the waiting room and into the lobby. The tall front doors framed a magnificent view of rolling green hills, interrupted here and there with the first colors of fall; fiery copper, bronze, and gold. Mike froze, staring at the beautiful sight. He loved autumn, loved flying his plane over the familiar Connecticut countryside, gazing at the palette of color below.

In three months the flaming beauty of autumn would be extinguished—and so would his life. Three months to live. September, October, November. It wasn't enough. He thought back three months, to June. It seemed like yesterday.

Suddenly Mike heard a burst of applause down the hall, and he remembered the piano. He followed the sound, curious to see the pianist who'd played the musical accompaniment to Dr. Bennett's tragic news.

16

"Am I too late for the concert?" he asked the receptionist. She consulted her watch.

"Well, yes, I'm afraid it's almost over, but Professor Brewster might play an encore. It's in the lounge on your right."

The huge lounge was crowded, with folding chairs and wheelchairs stuffed into every available space. Mike squeezed inside and found a place to stand along the rear wall beside a pretty blond nurse. He peered over the sea of heads and spotted the pianist, bowing stiffly beside an ebony piano.

Professor Brewster didn't look at all like Mike had envisioned. Instead of a distinguished, white-bearded gentleman in a tuxedo, he saw a prim-looking woman with a shapeless body, wearing a thick wool suit the color of mud. She was about his own age, Mike guessed, and wore her dark hair cut short. She had ramrod straight posture, and all the lines in her face seemed creased into a permanent frown. Mike unconsciously made a sour face in imitation.

"Is that Professor Brewster?" he asked the nurse in a stage whisper.

"Yes."

"Do you suppose she knows her piano's out of tune?"

"Shh . . ." Professor Brewster had begun to speak.

"Thank you, ladies and gentlemen. You've been most kind."

Her voice sounded cold and formal, and her smile looked stiff from lack of use. For some reason she

17

seemed vaguely familiar to Mike, and he tried to recall where they might have met.

"For my encore I will play a short piece by Bach." She pronounced the composer's name reverently, the way TV preachers said "God."

As the encore took off, Mike discovered that watching Professor Brewster play was much more interesting than listening to her through the wall. She sat stiffly on the bench, dangerously close to the edge, and glared at the piano like a general sizing up the enemy. Her long, tapered fingers poised motionlessly above the keyboard, then suddenly attacked like well-aimed missiles. The music rattled like a burst of machine-gun fire. A few moments later the music slowed and the professor used her fingers to caress each note, as if wooing the instrument, drawing soothing music from deep inside of it. Mike watched in fascination.

A few minutes later the encore ended and the audience burst into wild applause. Suddenly Mike realized why the professor looked familiar to him, and he laughed out loud. The blond nurse turned to him as if waiting for an explanation.

"Sorry," he said, chuckling. "It's just that the professor reminds me of a card game I once had as a kid. She looks like 'The Old Maid.'"

The nurse's eyes went wide. "Really, sir! Wilhelmina Brewster is on our Board of Directors! She's a professor of music at Faith College and a very distinguished citizen of our community!"

"Aw, I'm sorry, Ma'am." Mike smiled, as he touched her arm. "I didn't mean to insult the good professor. Forgive me?" When Mike Dolan smiled every line in his face came home where it belonged. No one could stay mad at him for very long.

"Oh, that's OK." The nurse smiled.

"So tell me something, Ma'am . . ." He leaned closer, whispering like a conspirator. ". . . is Professor Brewster married?"

The nurse glanced at the stiffly bowing professor, then covered her mouth to hide a smile. "Actually, no . . . she's not!" Mike held a finger to his lips and winked.

When the applause ended and the audience rose to leave, Mike waded through the crowd toward the piano. Professor Brewster greeted her audience as if they were fellow mourners at a funeral, shaking each hand somberly, her face grim. Mike waited in line, surprised by how tall she was up close—at least five inches taller than he was. When his turn came, he took her dry, limp hand and wrung it vigorously.

"Hi, Professor Brewster. I'm Mike Dolan. I enjoyed your encore, but do you know your piano's out of tune?"

Professor Brewster's eyebrows flew up, and her jaw fell down as if the puppeteer had suddenly dropped the strings. Someone behind him muttered, "How rude!" Mike hadn't meant to be. He hurried to remedy his error.

"I'm sorry. No offense, Ma'am. But if the Cancer

Center can't afford to get it fixed I'd be glad to kick in a little something to help out. I know they're always hard up for funds around here. Believe me, it'd be money well spent!"

Miss Brewster's gaze could have turned lava to stone. The corners of her mouth curved down in stern disapproval as she jerked her hand from Mike's enthusiastic grasp. How could he make her understand that he hadn't meant to insult her?

"Of course, I'm just an ordinary guy, and I don't know as much about music as you do, I'm sure. But the sound really grates on a fella's nerves, you know? Being out of tune and all? Especially when I was sitting next door in the doctor's office finding out that I'm going to die in three or four months. It probably bothers a lot of other people over there too." Mike smiled broadly, but the professor's forbidding expression never changed.

"OK, then, how about this, Professor? You hunt down a good mechanic and give me a call." He fumbled in the front pocket of his work shirt. "Here's my card. Call me, and I'll send you some money to help you pay for it."

She made no attempt to take his card, and Mike finally stuffed it into the pocket of her suit coat. He started to leave, then turned back.

"Oh, yeah, and in the meantime, give a dying man one last request . . . don't let anybody play on this thing until it's fixed up, OK?" He reached behind her and shut the keyboard lid with a soft, melodic slam.

The strings seemed to shudder with relief. "Bye." Mike tipped his cap to her and headed for the airport to grab some sky.

Professor Wilhelmina Brewster walked briskly out the door of the Cancer Center. She had no reason to hurry, but the lifelong habit could not be changed. As she marched to her car, oblivious to her surroundings and the beautiful fall afternoon, she reviewed every note of the piano recital she had just performed. She had played well.

As Wilhelmina stepped off the curb to cross to the parking lot, a convertible suddenly roared past, startling her. It was filled with young people, some in Faith College sweatshirts, honking the horn and singing the college football song. Wilhelmina's pleasant mood vanished. Resentment boiled within her at these strangers in the loud convertible for reminding her of a place she wanted to be but didn't belong, a place that was so much a part of her but where she wasn't wanted anymore. The car turned the corner in a flurry of fallen leaves.

For Wilhelmina, fall had always been a fulfilling time; preparing lectures, planning recitals, advising students, hearing auditions, and rushing to complete her much-too-busy schedule. But not this year. After 41 years as professor of music at Faith College, she had turned 65 last spring, the age of mandatory retirement.

She unlocked her blue Buick sedan and got in. The

vinyl upholstery was hot from the afternoon sunshine. The seven-year-old car still smelled new. She started the engine with a surge of hope. There must be some-place she had to be: a Connecticut League for Life meeting, the Ladies' Missionary Society, her weekly Bible study, the Garden Club? But there was no place to go except home, nowhere she was needed or wanted. She felt tears filling her eyes and was ashamed of herself. She had always been so strong, so proud of her independence. Why had she become so emotional lately?

She shut off the engine and reached in her pocket for a tissue. Instead, she found a business card. It had a picture of an airplane in the corner and bright blue let-tering:

Michael G. Dolan
Dolan and Sons Aviation
Cargo and Commuter Flights
Private Instruction

She stared at the card for a moment, unable to imagine where it had come from, then she remem-bered the rude little man at the recital who had told her the piano was out of tune. As if it had been *her* fault! Everyone knows that a pianist plays whatever instru-ment is available! A piano can't be tuned on the spot like a violin or a harp!

She replayed the scene in her mind, searching for an appropriately scathing reply she might have given him. At the time, his rudeness had rendered her speechless. What else had he said? ". . . only three or four months to live . . . give a dying man one last request . . ."

She dismissed the incident with a sigh. She didn't like to think about it, but there had probably been many terminally ill patients in her audience today. In fact she became a volunteer after her own mother died of cancer several years earlier. She knew from experience what Mr. Dolan's last three or four months would be like. Did he know? Probably not. He'd seemed too cheerful about it all, not asking for pity. The truth probably hadn't hit him yet. He was still in denial. But when that stage ended . . .

Tears welled up in her eyes again, and she scolded herself for them as she dug in her purse for a hanky. "Really, Wilhelmina! Such foolishness!"

She remembered smiling through Dean Bradford's long farewell speech at her retirement banquet last spring, putting on a brave show, disguising her unbearable pain as he'd severed her from the life she loved.

"Of course, this isn't good-bye," the dean had said. "As part of our faculty emeritus, I'm sure Professor Brewster will be called upon often for her wisdom and experience."

He'd hinted that he might win her an exemption from the mandatory retirement policy and keep her on the faculty part-time, but it hadn't happened. They'd bypassed her when they'd formed a search committee to hire her replacement. Her name hadn't appeared on the jury list to audition incoming freshmen for scholarship funds. And the invitation to the president's annual fall faculty party had never arrived. She had smiled bravely as if it hadn't hurt at all, just as Mr. Dolan smiled this afternoon. But now the campus had returned to life, a new semester was well underway, and for the first time in 41 years Wilhelmina wasn't part of it. A confident, young Ph.D. candidate probably sat in her office, filling her shelves with his books, while she sat here, alone. She had given her life to Faith College, and they had taken it, leaving her with nothing but a small pension and a few farewell gifts.

In many ways she was dying, too, just like Michael G. Dolan, except that Mr. Dolan would soon rest in peace while she would be forced to go on living an empty existence. She blew her nose on the lace-edged hanky. Yes, the truth had finally hit home.

She started the engine again and put the car into gear, driving the long way home instead of cutting across the campus. Her house, a stately, two-story Georgian brick, looked cold and dark in the fall afternoon light. She drove to the end of the curving driveway, past her formal flower beds and rosebushes. She was proud of her gardens. Most of her neighbors hired part-time gardeners or landscaping services, but Wilhelmina loved tending her flowers nearly as much as playing the piano. Weeding, fertilizing, and careful pruning had kept her busy most of the summer, but the

24

first frost in a couple of weeks would soon deprive her of this joy as well.

She pulled the car into the garage and walked around front to check the mailbox, hoping to find a letter with the familiar Faith College letterhead. They should have discovered their mistake by now. They would apologize for their oversight and ask her to return. But the only thing in the mailbox was a flyer: "Back to School Special; $2 off a large pizza with campus I.D. card." She unlocked the front door and angrily tossed the flyer in the hall wastebasket.

As she wandered into her huge formal living room and switched on the lights, it seemed as if she had just left home a few minutes ago for her recital. Her polished cherry-wood furniture reflected the glow, but the room still felt dark to her. Maybe she should have the Oriental rugs and draperies cleaned. A fine sheen of dust coated the grand piano, but she resisted the urge to brush it away with her hand, knowing it would damage the finish. She stuck her finger into the soil of her African violets in the bay window. They needed water. Maybe she should clean her entire house from top to bottom and fill the long winter days ahead with hard work. Her older brother had advised her to find something to occupy her time this winter. But what could ever replace her teaching career?

Wilhelmina put a Chopin etude on the stereo, then abruptly shut it off again after the opening notes. One of her students had played that etude at his recital last spring. How long would it take for the memories to fade? How long until she could listen to a recording or attend a concert without feeling such terrible pain?

The clock told her it was suppertime, but she didn't feel hungry. She picked at a little leftover salad, ate half a muffin, then dumped a pot of stale coffee down the drain. Wearily, she checked the memos she had written to herself and tacked to the refrigerator with magnetic quarter notes. She found nothing scheduled for tonight. Or tomorrow either, for that matter.

Suddenly the phone rang and she hurried to answer it, hoping to hear Dean Bradford's familiar voice offering her an end to this empty existence.

"Hello, Wilhelmina? This is Carol. How are you?"

Disappointment and rage brought tears to Wilhelmina's eyes, choking off her reply.

"I'm calling to remind you about the meeting this Friday at the Cancer Center. We're going to get the addresses of new patients to contact next week and—"

"I already know about the meeting, Carol."

"Well, I'm supposed to call everyone, you know. I'm just doing my job."

"I'm sorry," Wilhelmina said, blinking away her tears. "Do you need a ride on Friday? I can pick you up." Carol always needed a ride.

"Yes, if you don't mind, dear. OK then, I'll see you Friday. Bye-bye."

Wilhelmina checked make sure the date was marked on her calendar, glad to see at least one of the huge blank spaces filled in. September's photograph showed a weathered, one-room schoolhouse beneath an oak tree in fall foliage. The inspirational verse reminded her to "Rejoice in the Lord always."

Now what was that supposed to mean? How could she rejoice when they'd ripped her life away from her against her will? Rejoice in the *Lord?* She'd sacrificed her entire life for God, but He didn't seem to care about her anymore or even answer her prayers! She tore the picture off the top of the calendar, crushed it between her hands, and threw it across the room. Then Wilhelmina Brewster sank down at the table, laid her head on her arms, and wept.

2

Tuesday, September 8, 1987

Mike Dolan studied his reflection in the bathroom mirror as he shaved. He'd lost more weight, but at least his face still looked tanned and healthy. He would tell his son Steve that he was on a diet. After all, he could stand to lose a little weight. He patted the slight belly that still hung over his belt. His family would never have to know the truth.

He heard the rumble of a jet engine overhead and looked at his watch. Like a sailor navigating by the stars, Mike timed his daily routine by the passenger jets that roared over his house on their way to and from Hartford Airport, 25 miles away. This United commuter jet to Washington told him it was almost time to leave for work.

He switched off the bathroom light and went into the hallway. He could see his entire house at once from here. In the tiny, crowded living room on his right there were cobwebs on the moose antlers and dust on his bowling trophies. The bear skin rug needed a pass with the vacuum. Newspapers and aviation magazines lay scattered everywhere. In the bedroom on his left he saw his unmade bed. Small mounds of dirty laundry decorated that room, along with still more aviation magazines. Behind him in the kitchen, a pile of dishes in the sink threatened to topple over. He knew he should tidy up. But Buster and Heinz, his canine roommates, sat expectantly at his feet, tails thumping on the hardwood floor.

They were big dogs, too big for his tiny bungalow, and every time they moved they swept something off an end table or shelf with their bushy, wagging tails, leaving a trail of disaster and dog hair in their wake. Buster, who was mostly golden retriever, had an amiable personality, opening his heart to friend and stranger alike. Heinz, a black and white mutt of "57 varieties," served as the watchdog of the pair, more cautious and protective of his home and master.

"Ah, let's skip the cleaning," Mike told them. "We can take care of this place tomorrow, right guys? Let's go to the park and walk through the leaves." Buster sprang up and raced to the back door, tail wagging. Heinz gave a woof of approval. "OK, that settles it.

28

Let me call Stevie first." He dialed the familiar number on the wall phone in the kitchen.

"Hi, Cheryl, is Steve there? Oh . . . he left already, huh? OK, I'll catch him later at the hangar. Hey, give those kids a kiss from Grandpa, OK? Bye."

As he reached for his jacket, the dogs suddenly tore past him again, heading for the front door, barking a warning. In seconds the doorbell rang.

"OK, guys, OK! You did your job, now quiet down!" he had to shout above the noise. The barking continued, each dog trying to outdo the other.

Mike opened the door, then froze in astonishment. Professor Brewster—the piano lady—stood on his front porch! She looked equally astonished to see him, and for a moment neither of them could speak. Buster broke the impasse by leaping against the tattered screen door, barking a friendly greeting. Behind him, Heinz growled a more menacing alarm. Professor Brewster and the frail-looking woman beside her backed up a few steps. Mike tugged on Buster's collar.

"Get down, you big horse! You're scaring these nice people half to death! It's OK, ladies," he shouted above the din. "They're just being friendly. They won't hurt anybody." He grabbed Heinz's collar with his other hand and pointed both dogs toward the kitchen. "Go on, guys . . . go lay down." The dogs crept into the kitchen like guilty schoolboys headed for the principal's office. Mike held the screen door open.

"Come on in, ladies. It's great to see you again, Professor. You get that piano tuned up yet?"

"We're not here about the piano, Mr. Dolan." Her expression was somber, as if she'd come to deliver news of a terrible disaster.

Mike turned to the second woman and got a totally different impression. Her face glowed as if she'd come to tell him he'd won the lottery. With her feathery gray hair and quick, birdlike movements, she posed a humorous contrast to the tall, scholarly professor, like a twittering sparrow beside a gloomy owl.

"Hello, I'm Carol Nugent. We're here representing the hospice program. Can we have a few minutes of your time?"

"Sure! Sure! C'mon in!" Heinz barked in protest from the kitchen. Mrs. Nugent hesitated on the doorstep.

"Oh, dear . . . maybe I'd better not. I'm terribly allergic to dogs, you see."

The professor glared at her as if she were a piano student who'd played a wrong note. "Really, Carol. This will only take a few minutes."

"Well . . . all right, but . . ."

Mike held the door open for them as they stepped gingerly into the living room. He watched them take in the cluttered surroundings. He wished he had tidied up.

"Sorry about the mess—," he began, but a violent sneeze from Mrs. Nugent interrupted him.

"Oh, dear," she moaned, as her hanky fluttered around her nose.

30

"Won't you ladies sit down?" Mike whisked a T-shirt and three magazines off the sofa and kicked a pair of socks out of sight beneath the lopsided coffee table.

The ladies sat down as another sneeze overwhelmed Mrs. Nugent. It was followed by a pitiful, "Oh, dear," and more hanky flutters. Mike parked on a footstool nearby.

"We represent the Cancer Society's hospice program," Mrs. Nugent began, wiping her nose. "Have you heard of it before?" Mike shook his head. Mrs. Nugent sneezed. "We're a volunteer group, working with cancer patients and their families and—" She paused to sneeze three times in a row, which seemed to be more than the professor could tolerate.

"Really, Carol! Perhaps you'd better wait in the car. I'll take care of this." She snatched the brochures and clipboard away from her as Mrs. Nugent excused herself with another sneeze and fled to the car.

The professor cleared her throat. "As Mrs. Nugent was saying, we're a volunteer group, working with cancer patients and their families. We received your name from Dr. Bennett's office."

She paused to slap a shiny brochure down on the table in front of him. Mike picked it up and glanced at the picture, then set it down again, strategically hiding a half-eaten bologna sandwich.

"Our hospice program offers support services to you and your family—transportation to therapy appointments, meals for those on special diets, help with housekeeping . . ." Her gaze flickered around the room. ". . . things of that nature. We also have clergymen and counselors on staff if you or your family require spiritual help and so forth."

Mike felt a wave of pity for stuffy Professor Brewster. She seemed very ill at ease with people, especially those who were terminally ill. He guessed that the delicate Mrs. Nugent usually did most of the talking. He smiled warmly to put the professor at ease, but her dour expression never changed. He remembered reading somewhere that it took more facial muscles to frown than to smile and briefly considered sharing that news with her.

"We also offer practical help with home nursing care," she continued, "for any patients who may require it in the later stages of their illness. And of course we have patient support groups where you and your family can meet and talk with other cancer patients and their families." She fidgeted on the lumpy sofa, moving closer to the edge as if eager to finish. "I can help you fill out this information sheet if you'd like me to, Mr. Dolan. It would give us a better idea what your specific needs might be." She flourished a pen and clicked it open.

"Well, I appreciate your coming all the way out here, Professor, but to tell you the truth, I don't think I'll be needing all these services . . . even though you probably think this place could use a housekeeper . . ."

"Perhaps your family would be interested in our programs, Mr. Dolan."

"Well, they don't exactly know that I'm dying, yet, and I'd just as soon keep it that way. You see, all the family I have is my son Steve, his wife, Cheryl, and their three kids. My oldest boy died in Vietnam and my wife, Helen, died 17 years ago. So I want my remaining time with them to be like it always was, you know? Not all misty and sad because I'm dying. I can't stand everyone feeling sorry for me and all that."

From Professor Brewster's reaction, Mike guessed he had played a whole bunch of wrong notes.

"Your family has a right to know about your illness, Mr. Dolan. Besides, you can't disguise your condition forever. Your son should do his part to take care of your needs."

"Oh, I know Steve would be glad to do whatever he could. He helped me take care of Helen when she was dying of cancer. But that's just what I'm hoping to avoid. My wife was sick an awful long time, and even though we loved her very much it was terribly hard on everyone to watch her suffer."

"That's where hospice can help you. And your son as well."

"You know what? You get to the point with loved ones where they're suffering so much you just wish they could die. Then you feel guilty for wishing it. I can't put Stevie through that ordeal again. Or Cheryl and my grandkids either."

"There is always Mercy Hospital, which specializes in care for the terminally ill. You don't have to burden your family."

33

"Ma'am, I don't want to die hooked up to a bunch of tubes and gadgets. Would you?"

"Well . . . I really . . ."

"Listen, Professor, my oldest son, Mikey Jr., was a chopper pilot. He flew Huey Cobras over in Nam picking up wounded and flying them to aid stations. He saved a lot of lives. When his chopper was shot down, he died instantly . . ." Mike snapped his fingers, ". . . but he died *living,* you know what I mean? Living life to the fullest, right up to the end. That's what I want to do too . . . die *living!*" She stared at him without answering. Mike couldn't tell if she understood.

"Look, I know my old body is all full of cancer, but I still feel pretty good right now. So I'm just going to keep on living like I always have and not let on to Stevie that anything's wrong. Then when the time comes and the cancer starts winning the fight, well, I guess I'll just take the Cessna up one day and forget to land her again."

Professor Brewster reacted as if she'd been struck. "Mr. Dolan! You wouldn't end your own life!"

"Well, the doctor says my life is about to end anyway. What difference will a few days or weeks make?"

"I think you need to discuss this with your clergyman right away!"

Mike laughed. "An old sinner like me? I can't say that I know any clergymen who'd talk to me."

"Well, hospice has many denominations represented

on our staff. I'd be happy to arrange an appointment with a pastor or a priest . . ." Mike patted her shoulder to calm her, but she stiffened at his touch. He quickly retreated.

"I do appreciate your concern, Ma'am, and I'm sorry if I've shocked you. But I've thought this all out, and I know it's the best thing I could do for my family. My grandkids will accept my death a lot better knowing I died in the cockpit, doing what I love the most."

Professor Brewster stood abruptly and brushed the dog hair from her dark wool skirt. "I really must go."

Her reaction puzzled him. Mike hadn't intended to tell anyone about his final plans. They had just slipped out. But he couldn't understand why she seemed so upset. If he was going to die anyway, what did it matter when or how? He followed her to the door.

"The hospice phone number is on the brochure if you decide to call us, Mr. Dolan."

"OK, thanks . . . and hey, I hope you won't tell anybody what we . . . uh . . . talked about, Professor."

"Of course not. Good day." The screen door banged behind her as she marched to the car.

"Hey, Professor!" Mike opened the door again and shouted after her. "Don't forget the piano!" She got into the car as if she hadn't heard.

Mike walked out to the kitchen, shaking his head. He never had been very good at figuring out women. His dogs scrambled to their feet. "OK, guys. Let's go for that walk."

Wilhelmina gripped the steering wheel and drove through the swirling leaves as if pursued by terrorists. Coming face-to-face again with that rude little man from the piano recital had surprised her. But what he'd revealed to her about his plans to commit suicide had left her deeply shaken. She barely heard what Carol was saying to her.

". . . and I'm really sorry for running out on you, dear, but my goodness, I just couldn't stop sneezing in there! All that dog hair. And that horrible black rug too. What do you suppose it was? A dead bear? Anyway, I just couldn't help myself. It was dusty in there, too, wasn't it? I hope Mr. Dolan signed up for housekeeping services . . ."

Wilhelmina stomped on the accelerator, wishing she could tell Carol to be quiet. What did a little dust matter when Mr. Dolan planned to kill himself! It was too horrible to think about. Wilhelmina had never faced anything like this in her life, but Carol barely paused for breath.

"Did you get the forms all filled out and everything, dear? I really hated to leave you all alone but—" Wilhelmina swerved suddenly to avoid a slower-moving car and Carol gasped. "Good heavens, Wilhelmina! Why are you driving so fast?"

Wilhelmina didn't answer.

Suicide! She tried not to picture Mr. Dolan hanging from the rafters in his basement or grimly swallowing an overdose of pills beside his bathroom sink or putting a loaded gun to his temple.

"Why are you turning here, Wilhelmina? This isn't the way to—"

"I know. I'm taking you home."

"Home? . . . but we have three more patients to visit."

"I'm not feeling well. Couldn't we visit them tomorrow?"

"Well, I suppose we could, but . . . listen, are you upset with me or something? You've hardly said two words to me since we left that last home, and now you want to quit? I'm sorry I couldn't stop sneezing—"

"I'm not mad at you. It wasn't your fault."

"Well, what's wrong, then? Did that last man give you a hard time or something? He seemed like such a nice person."

Wilhelmina pulled up in front of Carol's house, stepping on the brakes a little harder than she intended to. She left the engine running. "Can we talk about it some other time, Carol? I need to go home and lie down."

"Sure . . . OK . . . I'll call you." The moment Carol closed the door Wilhelmina stomped on the accelerator and the car roared away. She caught a glimpse of Carol in the rearview mirror, standing on the curb, staring after her, wide-eyed. Wilhelmina knew she owed Carol an explanation or an apology but not now. Not while she was so upset. She had to talk to someone about this but certainly not Carol Nugent. Carol could spread a story faster than Wilhelmina could dial the phone.

Suicide. The thought of it chilled her. Maybe she should talk to the hospice director. But what about her promise to Mr. Dolan not to say anything? As she drove blindly through the streets wondering what to do, she suddenly thought of her pastor. He would never betray a confidence. She could give him Mr. Dolan's name and address, and the pastor would know exactly what to say to him. She turned at the next corner and drove straight to her church.

"Is Pastor Stockman in, please?" she asked the church secretary. "I don't have an appointment, but I'd like to speak with him for a moment, if I may."

"He's on the phone right now, Professor Brewster, but I don't think he'll be long. Why don't you have a seat."

Wilhelmina was too distraught to sit. She paced the length of the reception area several times until Pastor Stockman finally appeared at his office door and invited her in. The pastor was a tall, distinguished looking man in his early 50s with receding black hair and a beard salted with gray. He had a gracious, kindly manner and spoke with such an air of spiritual wisdom that he reminded Wilhelmina of one of the Old Testament patriarchs or prophets. He led her into his spacious office where hundreds of books lined the walls; everything from commentaries and concordances to counseling and cults. Wilhelmina began speaking before she'd even taken her seat.

"A most upsetting incident occurred today, Pastor. I simply must discuss it with someone, and I knew you'd understand the need to keep it confidential."

The pastor sank into the chair behind his enormous desk and nodded somberly. "Of course."

"I just visited a man for the Cancer Society's hospice program. A terminal cancer patient. In the course of our conversation he confided in me that he wouldn't be needing hospice's services because he plans to end his own life!"

The pastor sat forward abruptly. "Oh, my!"

"I think you can see why I'm so upset. We both feel the same way about euthanasia. As members of the Connecticut League for Life we can't simply look the other way when someone is planning suicide. But I don't know what to do. He has actually admitted that he intends to kill himself."

"I can certainly understand why you're upset, Miss Brewster."

"I was hoping that *you* could stop him, somehow, Pastor. I realize I can't report him anywhere, can I? Because of client confidentiality?"

"Hmm . . . that's probably true . . ." Pastor Stockman stroked his beard thoughtfully. He always spoke slowly, as if considering every word carefully before answering, a habit that drove impatient people like Wilhelmina crazy and made an appointment with him seem interminable.

"Do you know if he's a member of any church?" he finally asked. "Maybe you could speak to his own pastor or priest."

"He said he didn't have a church affiliation or a

pastor. I offered to refer him to one of our hospice clergymen, but he refused."

He paused. "Hmm . . . you don't think he's a Christian, then?"

"Well, I have to assume not. And that makes matters even worse, doesn't it, if he does commit suicide?"

The pastor stared thoughtfully at the ceiling for a moment, as if the answer he sought was encoded in the tiny dots of the ceiling tiles. "Does he have a specific plan to end his life, Miss Brewster, or were these just vague threats?"

Wilhelmina thought for a moment. What had Mr. Dolan said? Something about taking off in his airplane and forgetting to land again.

"No, it's not a vague threat. He seems to have it all planned."

"Hmm . . ." The flashing red light on Pastor Stockman's telephone ticked off the seconds noiselessly. Finally he leaned forward. "Do you think this could just be a manifestation of self-pity? It would be natural for him to feel hopeless if he recently found out that he's terminally ill. Thoughts of suicide are often an initial reaction to news of this nature. Did he seem emotionally upset to you?"

Both times she'd talked to Mike Dolan he'd been smiling. He seemed to be at peace with the world as he calmly plotted to do what he thought was best for his family. If he were only pretending to be undisturbed, he was a very convincing actor.

"No, he didn't appear to be upset," she said. "In fact,

he seemed quite calm about it all." Wilhelmina opened her purse and rummaged through it. "I have his card here, somewhere. Couldn't you talk to him, Pastor?"

Rev. Stockman shook his head. "I can't drop by his home uninvited. This is a very delicate situation, Miss Brewster."

"Oh dear. Then there's nothing we can do?"

"Well, I think someone should talk with him again. And since you've established the initial contact with him, I think it should be you."

Wilhelmina's eyes grew wide. "*Me?* I'm not a minister or a trained counselor!" The thought of returning to Mr. Dolan's shabby little house repulsed her.

"I understand your fears, Miss Brewster. But you are a fine Christian woman, and I'm sure that God can help you find a way to share the gospel with this man. If he accepts Christ, you see, he may decide not to kill himself after all."

Wilhelmina shuddered. She couldn't possibly do it. She had felt rebuffed when Mr. Dolan rejected the offer of hospice services. The thought of offering him the gospel of Jesus Christ to reject was unthinkable.

"Did he leave an opening for you to visit him again?" the pastor prodded. "I know it's difficult to go where you're unwelcome, but can you think of a valid reason to talk to him?"

The out-of-tune piano. Mr. Dolan couldn't stop fussing about it. It would be a reasonable excuse to see him again. Wilhelmina knew it was her Christian duty to help Mr. Dolan find Christ. But she simply did not want to do it. She had come to the church hoping to dump Mike Dolan in the pastor's lap and forget about him. Now she found herself in the uncomfortable position of explaining to her evangelical pastor that she wanted no part in winning Mr. Dolan's eternal soul. She had never witnessed to anyone in her life. She was a musician. Her ministry to the Body of Christ was music, not evangelism.

"I'll have to give it some thought," she said, as she rose to leave. "I might run into him again at the Cancer Center. Thank you for your time, Pastor. I know you're busy."

"You're very welcome. I'm sorry I couldn't be of more help to you. But please, let me know how this works out, all right?"

Wilhelmina felt worse than before. She hurried back to her car and stormed out of the parking lot, the gravel spitting beneath her tires. As she roared past the front of the church the words on the message board struck her like a rebuke:

I am the resurrection and the life. He who believes in me will live, even though he dies (John 11:25).

Wilhelmina knew she could never witness to Mike Dolan. She had no idea what to say to someone like him or how to say it. But someday soon she would undoubtedly read a story in the newspaper about his death in an airplane crash. How would she live with her guilt when she did?

3

Tuesday, September 15, 1987

Wilhelmina stared out of the parsonage window, watching golden maple leaves drift lazily to the ground one by one. She ached with restlessness, longing for something useful to do and somewhere else to go besides this sleepy women's Bible study led by Pastor Stockman's wife, Ellen. Wilhelmina would have considered it a waste of time if she hadn't had so much time to waste.

She'd only attended afternoon Bible study classes since the beginning of September, but already she found them dull. Her faith and her relationship with Christ were deeply personal, and she disliked sharing details of them with anyone else. She also hated trying to fill in the correct responses in the study booklet, as if the answers to all the questions of life could be stuffed into those tiny blank spaces. Real life seldom came with simple answers.

These classes were designed for lonely old ladies with nothing better to do, not for Wilhelmina Brewster. At least not until this year. How she missed the youthful energy of her college students, their enthusiasm and zest for life. She had often caught them gazing out of the window on beautiful days like today, paying little attention to her lectures on baroque and renaissance music, and probably wishing they were outside on the college lawn with their friends. For the first time in her life, Wilhelmina understood how they'd felt.

She took a sip of lukewarm coffee and leaned back on the sofa. Mrs. Stockman had decorated the cozy living room of the parsonage with Bible verse plaques and olive wood souvenirs from the Holy Land and furnished it comfortably with plump sofas and chairs. It was a haven of calm, with everything neatly organized, carefully dusted, and smelling of potpourri. Except for the slightly worn rugs, no one would ever guess that the Stockmans had raised three sons in this house.

Seated beside Wilhelmina, Carol Nugent had her Bible open to Exodus, chapters 3 and 4. Wilhelmina found the same place in her own Bible, then opened her study booklet to today's lesson.

She stared in horror. The answer blanks were all empty! She had forgotten to do her homework or read the lesson ahead of time. All her life she'd prided herself on her efficiency. Why had she suddenly become so careless and unorganized? She detested those attributes in others.

She stole a peek at Mrs. Stockman to see if she'd noticed the barren pages, but Ellen was chatting happily about the lesson and paying no attention to Wilhelmina. The pastor's wife was a pretty, plumpish woman with graying blond hair and a warm, welcoming smile. She seemed to have been born with a sweet disposition, and Wilhelmina couldn't imagine Ellen losing her temper or kicking the family dog. A dozen markers stuck out of Ellen's Bible, and her graceful writing spilled out of the answer blanks into the margins of her booklet. She clearly enjoyed her role as teacher, but Wilhelmina felt uncomfortably out of place as a student.

Wilhelmina tilted her study guide upright to conceal her crime and glanced at today's lesson title: "Saying Yes to God." She made a face. She didn't care to say *anything* to God and recognized, with a start, that she was mad at Him. Mad at God! She'd served Him faithfully for 41 years at the college, giving up everything else to make teaching her whole life, but God had snuffed out that life as quickly and thoroughly as candles on a birthday cake. All He'd offered her in place of teaching was this sleepy Bible study and charitable volunteer work, poor substitutes indeed for her life as a college professor. Yes, she was angry at God.

She swallowed the remainder of her tepid coffee and leaned forward to place the cup on a coaster, determined to concentrate on the lesson in spite of her lingering bitterness.

"God may not always take 'no' for an answer," Mrs. Stockman was saying. "We'll see in this passage how many times Moses tried to avoid God's calling on his life. Let's go around the circle, shall we, ladies? And each take a turn reading?" She nodded toward the woman on her right, who began to read:

45

"Moses said to God, 'Who am I, that I should go to Pharaoh and bring the Israelites out of Egypt?'"

For some bizarre reason the verse reminded Wilhelmina of Mike Dolan. Moses' words seemed to echo her defiant protest to Pastor Stockman; *"I'm not a minister or a trained counselor!"* She blushed at the memory, then glanced at her watch. Forty-five minutes until freedom.

Time dragged ponderously by. Mrs. Stockman seemed to teach in slow motion. Wilhelmina's attention wandered as the ladies talked on and on. Her jaw ached from stifling yawns.

". . . Even after all these promises," Mrs. Stockman said, "how did Moses answer God?"

One of the women in the circle read: "What if they do not believe me or listen to me . . . ?"

Wilhelmina shifted uncomfortably on the sofa. Once again she had the uncanny feeling that Moses' attitude toward Pharaoh resembled her attitude toward Mike Dolan. Their reactions had been too similar; "I couldn't possibly do it!" The room felt hot and stuffy. She stared out of the window.

Carol Nugent read next: "And Moses said, 'O Lord, I have never been eloquent. . . . I am slow of speech and tongue.'"

"And my ministry is in music, not evangelism!" Wilhelmina wanted to shout.

Mrs. Stockman smiled sweetly at Wilhelmina. "But God assured Moses that He would help him, didn't He?" she said.

46

Wilhelmina's heart pounded. Why were her hands shaking? She stared at her lap, afraid that her guilty conscience was evident, like the blackened tongue of a naughty child who had pilfered her grandmother's licorice. Wilhelmina heard the animated discussion, but the words were unintelligible to her. She wished she could go home. Suddenly the room grew still. She looked up.

"Professor Brewster, it's your turn," Ellen Stockman said. "Read verses 12 and 13, please." Wilhelmina gripped her Bible tightly and cleared her throat.

" 'Now go; I will help you speak and will teach you what to say.' But Moses said, 'O Lord, please send someone else to do it.' "

She nearly choked on the words.

These verses were more than a 4,000-year-old dialogue between Moses and God. Wilhelmina felt the overwhelming conviction that God was speaking to her. He was commanding her to go to Mike Dolan just as He'd commanded Moses to go to Pharaoh. And, like Moses, she was responding to God with excuses, telling Him to send someone else.

If only she had someone to talk to about all of this. She didn't dare go back to Pastor Stockman and confess her failures and misgivings, much less admit to him that she was angry at God. She was the church organist, for goodness sake. What would he think of her? And Mrs. Stockman seemed sweetly oblivious to the harsh realities of suicide and terminal illness.

She had the urge to confide in Carol Nugent, just to get everything off her chest, but Carol's biggest weakness was her prying curiosity. Wilhelmina knew her friend would never be content until she had extracted the whole story from her, including Mr. Dolan's terrible plan to end his own life. No, she couldn't talk to Carol.

She looked down at her Bible, curious to see what God's response had been when Moses refused his assignment. The next verse read: "Then the LORD'S anger burned against Moses."

Wilhelmina had learned this familiar story ages ago, in Sunday School. She knew that in the end Moses went to Pharaoh. It was one thing to be mad at God and quite another to have Him mad at you. She could feel the heat of God's anger now, as real as any burning bush. The fire would probably blaze hotter and hotter until she finally agreed to go to Egypt and talk to Pharaoh—or Mike Dolan.

All around Wilhelmina, ladies were closing their Bibles and zipping them shut, stuffing them in purses and tote bags. The Bible study was over at last.

"As we close in silent prayer today," Mrs. Stockman said, "let's examine our hearts for any area of our lives where we may be saying 'no' to God."

Wilhelmina bowed her head. For several long minutes she wrestled with her lingering bitterness, unable to pray.

"OK, Lord," she finally managed. "I suppose I can think of *some* way to talk to Mr. Dolan again. But

You'll have to help me. I am certainly not very good at this."

"Amen," Mrs. Stockman said. "Thank you for coming, ladies. And remember, if you say 'yes' to God, He'll help you accomplish the task."

After she dropped off Carol, Wilhelmina began formulating a plan that would rid her conscience of Mr. Dolan with a minimum of effort. First she stopped at the Christian bookstore and purchased two tracts. *The Plan of Salvation* had a picture on the cover of Jesus knocking on a door. The other pamphlet, ominously titled *Where Will You Spend Eternity?* showed a golden city in the clouds, high above a burning lake of fire and brimstone. The two tracts would spell out the whole story for Mr. Dolan. The choice to accept or reject Jesus would be his alone.

When she reached home she pulled out the phone book, anxious to complete her plan. First she called Anthony Amato, her piano tuner, and arranged to meet him at the Cancer Center tomorrow afternoon at two o'clock. Next she called the center to schedule the appointment with them. Finally, with a deep breath and a firm resolution, she took out Mr. Dolan's business card and dialed his number.

"Hello, Dolan Aviation." The sound of an engine droned in the background.

"Good afternoon. May I speak with Mr. Dolan, please?"

"Sure. Which one do you want?"

Wilhelmina looked down at the card. "Michael G. Dolan, please."

"Sure thing. Hang on . . . Hey, Dad! It's for you . . ." The engine shut off, and a few moments later Wilhelmina heard Mike's cheerful voice.

"This is Mike. How can I help you?"

"Hello, Mr. Dolan, this is Wilhelmina Brewster. I . . ."

"Well, hi there, Professor. How are you?"

"Very well, thank you. I'm calling about the piano at the Cancer Center and—"

"Hey, that's great! Did you get it all fixed up?"

She wished he would stop interrupting and allow her to finish, but she held her tongue. "My piano tuner is scheduled to go to the center tomorrow at 2 P.M. If you'd like to come and—"

"That would be great! I've never watched anyone tune up a piano before. Will you be there?"

"Yes, I plan to be there."

"Well, OK then. It's a date. See you at two tomorrow. Bye now."

Wilhelmina's hand shook as she replaced the receiver. The fact that he'd called their appointment a "date" made her uneasy, but it couldn't be helped. She placed the two tracts in her purse, along with a brochure about her church, and snapped it shut. Her plan was in motion. She'd meet him at 2:00, give him the pamphlets, and be free at last from any guilt concerning Michael G. Dolan's eternal soul.

By 1:30 the following afternoon Wilhelmina's nerves

felt as tightly stretched as piano wire. She had spent all morning dreading this appointment and, at the same time, anxiously waiting to get it over with—like going to the dentist to have an aching tooth pulled, she decided. Her palms were damp with sweat, and she had trouble pulling on the short gray gloves that matched her gray wool suit. She locked the front door, made sure the tracts were still in her purse, and was about to leave through the kitchen door when the phone rang. She let out a startled cry. This whole messy business had made her much too jittery. She snatched up the receiver.

"Oh, Professor Brewster, I'm glad I caught you. This is Angela Amato." She sounded breathless. "Tony won't be able to tune that piano for you today after all. He hurt his back this morning tuning a spinet."

"Oh no!" Wilhelmina closed her eyes. Now what was she supposed to do?

"He's at the chiropractor's right now, but he'll call you when he's ready to go back to work, maybe in a couple days. Those little spinets are so hard to tune, you know. Real back-breakers! I told him he should charge more, but he—"

"Thank you, Mrs. Amato. Have him call me when he's well again."

After she'd slammed the receiver down, Wilhelmina realized she hadn't offered any sympathy for the poor man. But there hadn't been time for it. She had to intercept Mr. Dolan before he made a trip to the

Cancer Center for nothing. She dug in her purse for his card, then dialed the number.

"Dolan Aviation. Good afternoon." Again, Wilhelmina heard the whine of engines in the background.

"May I speak with Mr. Michael Dolan, please."

"Sorry, Ma'am, he's not here. Left about 10 minutes ago. Said he'd be back around five."

Wilhelmina hung up the phone without even saying good-bye. Why were all her carefully laid plans going awry? It would be very awkward talking to Mr. Dolan now, without chatty Mr. Amato and the diversion of the piano being tuned. She'd have to confront him alone, and the memory of her last conversation with him filled her with dread. They came from two completely different worlds. They had absolutely nothing in common except the out-of-tune piano. Now they didn't even have that.

"Oh, confound it all!" she cried aloud. She could postpone this meeting, but then she would have to go through a long morning of worry and stress all over again. No. She wanted to give him the tracts and get it over with. But what on earth could they talk about?

Without warning, the words of Moses echoed through her mind, *"O Lord, I'm not eloquent . . . ,"* and her anger at God leaped to life like a brushfire. Of all the Christians in this city, why did God have to choose *her* to witness to Mr. Dolan? And how could a loving God wrench her career away from her? Wilhelmina could no longer control her tears, and that made her angrier still. She slammed the back door on her way out, stalked to her car, and drove blindly to the Cancer Center.

When Wilhelmina entered the lobby, Mike Dolan stood with his back to her, baseball cap in hand, chatting with the receptionist. He wore dark green work coveralls with the Dolan Aviation logo on the back. When he turned around to greet her she saw "Mike" embroidered in red above his front pocket.

"Hi, Professor, good to see you again." He smiled warmly and extended his hand. His clothes were neat, his hands clean, but a residual odor of engine oil seemed to trail in his wake.

"I tried to reach you earlier, Mr. Dolan, but you'd already left. Mr. Amato can't tune the piano today. He hurt his back this morning."

"Oh, I'm sorry to hear that. Is he going to be all right?"

"I expect so. Back problems are an occupational hazard for piano tuners."

"Is that right? I never knew that. Guess you learn something new every day."

"I'm sorry you had to waste a trip."

"Oh, that's no problem, Professor. My son's probably glad to have me out of his hair for a while."

Wilhelmina had no idea how to respond. There was an awkward silence. She wished she could simply shove the tracts in his hand and say good-bye, but that would be much too rude. Mike broke the silence first.

"Hey, Professor, how about a cup of coffee? There's a doughnut shop just down the block. I know you're probably a busy person and all, but as long as we're here . . ."

Wilhelmina couldn't imagine anything she'd enjoy less than sitting in a smoky doughnut shop beside Mr. Dolan in his embroidered work clothes. But since she had no other plan of action, she might as well accept his invitation. She glanced at her watch, pretending she was on a tight schedule.

"Well . . . I suppose I have time for a quick cup."

"Great! Let's go!" He waved good-bye to the receptionist and held the door open for Wilhelmina. They started down the street together.

"Sure has been great fall weather, eh, Professor?"

"Yes. It has."

"I love these warm days and cool nights, don't you?"

"Yes."

"Is this what they call 'Indian Summer'?"

"I'm not sure."

"I'll bet your students can hardly keep their minds on their lessons on a gorgeous day like today." He was soon breathless from trying to keep up with Wilhelmina's brisk pace. She forced herself to slow down.

"Actually, Mr. Dolan, I'm not teaching at the college anymore. I've retired."

"No way! You're too young for that!" He looked shocked, but she spotted a twinkle in his eye.

How cold and unfriendly her disposition must seem

to someone as good-natured as Mr. Dolan! Wilhelmina tried to justify their opposite moods by telling herself that he still had a job to go to every day while she had none. Then she remembered that he was terminally ill.

Wilhelmina drew a deep breath. She simply must try to be a little friendlier. After all, she was on an important mission. And besides, she'd never have to see him again after today.

"Yes, Mr. Dolan, it's true. I retired from teaching last spring after 41 years at Faith College."

"Well, that's great. So, do you have lots of plans now, with so much freedom? Travel around the world and all that?"

"No, I never cared much for traveling. I'm busy with my work for the Cancer Society. And my church, of course." She was pleased with herself for slipping religion into the conversation. It was a good beginning. But they had reached the doughnut shop, and by the time they took a seat at a greasy booth by the window the opportunity to witness had passed.

"We'd like two coffees," Mike told the waitress. "I'll have a grape jelly doughnut . . . and what'll you have, Professor?"

"I really don't care for anything."

"But these are the best doughnuts in town. Come on, try one."

When would this ever end? Greasy foods made Wilhelmina's gall bladder act up. But she ordered a plain doughnut to make him happy and to avoid a lengthy

explanation about her inner anatomy. After the waitress served their food, Wilhelmina struggled for a way
to bring their conversation back on course. Before she
could think of one, Mike started talking.

"Yes sir, I think retirement's the reward for a good
life well lived, don't you? So tell me, your volunteer
work can't keep you busy all the time. What else have
you got cooked up?"

Wilhelmina was at a loss for words. Most people her
age usually did make retirement plans, but she had
never dreamt that she would have to retire. If only she
hadn't relied on the dean's assurances that she could
teach part-time. If only he'd kept his promise . . .

"Sorry. I guess it's none of my business." When
Mike interrupted her thoughts Wilhelmina realized
that he had been waiting a long time for her answer.
She silently scolded herself for her atrocious manners
and decided to be honest with him.

"Actually, Mr. Dolan, I haven't made any plans. You
see, I loved teaching. It's all I've ever known. And I
didn't want to retire. I thought I might stay on at the
college part-time, but it didn't happen that way."

"That's a real shame, Professor . . . a talented lady
like yourself . . ." His eyes held hers, and she saw so
much sympathy and compassion in them that Wilhelmina's eyes filled with tears. He didn't turn away
in embarrassment. Instead, she had the feeling that he
was about to reach for her hand. She quickly folded
them in her lap.

"But even if that college is stupid enough to let you

go, there must be a dozen other places that'd be tickled to have you, Professor."

"I'm 65, Mr. Dolan. Most schools look for a much younger person."

"That's *dumb!*" He banged his fist on the table, causing the coffee cups to rattle. "You're not ready to be put out to pasture yet!"

"True. But it happened. Anyway, I'm not sure I'd be happy at another school. Faith was my alma mater, you see. Father taught at Faith College and the seminary, too, for ages and ages. My entire life has revolved around the college, I suppose."

"Does your family live around here?"

"My older brother, Laurentius, is senior pastor of a church up in Springfield, and my younger brother, Peter, is a professor of religious studies down at Yale."

"Wow! You're *all* a bunch of eggheads!"

Wilhelmina smiled in spite of herself. Her attitude toward him softened slightly. "No, not really. But Father always stressed the importance of a good education, and I guess we all took him seriously. After I graduated from Faith I earned a master of music degree from Hartford Conservatory, then took a job back here. I wouldn't know where else to teach even if they'd have me."

"Well then, how about your other lifelong dreams? What'd you always want to do when you were a kid that you never had a chance to do?"

He seemed so kind and so genuinely interested in her that Wilhelmina found it easy to be open with him.

"To be honest, Mr. Dolan, I don't remember dreaming of anything else. I remember piano lessons and recitals and practicing for music competitions and—"

"Did you win any?"

"Pardon me?"

"The competitions . . . did you win any of them?"

"Most of them, yes." She allowed herself to smile. "Father taught us how to set goals and how to work to achieve them."

"Well, I'm happy that you won . . . and I hope you won't take this wrong . . . but it all sounds pretty dull. How about time off to have fun? Doing kid stuff. You didn't have to practice piano all the time, did you?"

"Oh, but I enjoyed practicing! I never cared much for silly childhood games."

"Didn't you ever play hooky from school and go fishing? Explore a haunted house? Ride a toboggan? Fly a kite? Fun things like that?"

"Not that I recall . . . but I did have a happy childhood, Mr. Dolan. Truly." Why did she suddenly feel like she'd missed something in life? "Music has been my whole life, and I've been very content with it." *Until now,* she finished silently. She wondered how she ever started talking about herself and decided to steer the conversation back to him. "How about yourself, Mr. Dolan, do you enjoy music?"

Mike laughed, and it was an easy, rumbling sound, like a child toying with the low registers of a piano. "I enjoy certain kinds of music, but I don't know very much about your kind. I've never been to a symphony or a ballet or anything like that. And my dad never bugged me about getting an education like yours did. He had to work two shifts down in the shipyards just to keep food on our table, so we never saw much of him. There were seven of us kids, and we were on our own most of the time. Had some great times together. Got in some real scrapes too!" He laughed again.

"When did you become interested in flying?"

"When I was 13 or 14 I met a guy named Joe Donovan. He'd been a genuine World War I flying ace. Even fought against the famous Red Baron once. I used to spend hours down at the little airfield and Joe'd fill my ears with all his flying stories. Taught me a lot about planes too. Even taught me to fly one. Joe was some guy! Like a father to me. Anyhow, when the second war started heating up, I quit my job and signed up for the air force. They taught me to really fly . . . P51 Mustangs . . . bomber escorts. You know?"

Wilhelmina nodded, but the world he talked about was alien to her.

"I saved all my pay, even made a little extra on the side, and after the war I started buying scrap aircraft and fixing them up. Pretty soon I had my own little fleet. I worked a bush pilot operation for a while up in the Yukon, Northwest Territories, and Alaska. I could tell you some stories! Those were the days!"

He was quiet for a moment, but his face seemed to glow as he reminisced. Again, Wilhelmina was struck by how different their lives were, how very little they had in common.

Finally Mike sighed. "But after I got married and the kids came along . . . you know how it goes. Helen wanted to settle down back home. She couldn't take those northern winters. So, Dolan and Sons Aviation moved back here."

The waitress returned and silently refilled their cups. He took a few sips and finished his doughnut. "I asked you about your dreams, Professor, because I guess I've always had my own little dream. Ever since those days I spent with Joe Donovan I've always dreamed of owning a little fleet of antique planes, World War I types—Sopwith Camels, Spads, Fokkers. I'd like to fix them up and give air shows—mock dogfights, just like Eddie Rickenbacker and the Red Baron. Flying was really flying in those days. Now everything's computerized on modern fighter jets. All the fun's gone. But in those days it was man to man, machine to machine."

Wilhelmina was about to ask him why he didn't pursue his dream when she remembered why. She stared down at her hands, wrapped around her coffee mug, and tried to think of something to say.

"I guess flying is my reason for living, Professor, and music is yours. I love being up in the air more than I do being on the ground. Maybe I should have been a bird. You like to fly?"

"Me? I don't know . . . I've never flown."

"What? Never in your whole life?"

"No."

"Well, I can change that!" He leaped to his feet and

pried her hand off the coffee mug, taking it firmly in his own. "Come on, my favorite Cessna's all fueled up and ready to go. And this is the best time of year to fly too. You haven't seen a New England fall until you've seen it from the air!"

She pulled her hand free and stared at him. "I couldn't possibly go!"

"Why not? Don't tell me you're afraid to fly, Professor?"

Wilhelmina was too dumbfounded to answer. His face broke into a kindly grin.

"Ma'am, you're safer in my airplane than you are driving home today. Come on, give it a try. I promise we'll land safely again."

His blunt kindness unnerved her. This man had no facades or hidden agendas like so many of her colleagues in the academic world. Here she was, a virtual stranger, yet he'd offered to pop her into his airplane and fly her all over the countryside to see the fall leaves. He meant well, but it was out of the question.

"No, really. Thank you, but I can't." She checked her watch without seeing the time and rose to go.

"Well, if you change your mind, Professor, you can give me a shout anytime and I'll take you up, free of charge."

"That's kind of you, Mr. Dolan, but—"

"It's Mike. Call me Mike. And I'm serious about that offer, Professor." He paid for their coffee and doughnuts and left a generous tip.

Wilhelmina could find nothing to say as they walked back to the Cancer Center along the tree-lined street. Mike shuffled his feet through the fallen leaves, deliberately making them rustle, and the sound grated on Wilhelmina's nerves. The leaves looked ugly to her—dry, dead, useless things, cast-off and unwanted, fit only to be burned.

"Isn't that a beautiful sound, Professor?" Mike said suddenly. "The sounds of fall are one of my favorite kinds of music. You know what I read somewhere once? The leaves actually sacrifice themselves. They fall off the branches and die, just so the tree can survive the winter that's coming. Isn't that something?"

"Mm . . . yes," she mumbled. How could he be so perpetually, unceasingly cheerful, especially under the circumstances? Wilhelmina's own depression weighed so heavily on her that she could barely get out of bed in the mornings. At night, she'd lie awake unable to sleep.

When they reached the center she turned to him. "Thank you for the coffee, Mr. Dolan. I'm sorry about the piano and the wasted trip."

"Not at all, not at all! I enjoyed talking with you. You take care, now, and I'll be waiting to hear from you whenever you decide to take your first flight. Bye now." He waved his baseball cap in salute and disappeared around the corner.

Wilhelmina walked slowly to her car, rustling the leaves with her feet, trying in vain to hear the "music."

When she opened her purse to get her car keys, she saw the two tracts. For the first time in her entire life, Wilhelmina swore.

4

Saturday, September 19, 1987

Mike hummed a country-western tune along with the car radio as he pulled his aging pickup truck into his son's driveway. He tooted the horn and the door of the ranch-style house burst open. Three children rushed out, laughing and shouting all at once.

"Where are the kites, Grandpa? Did you get the kites?"

From the back of the truck, Buster and Heinz joined in the tumult with a chorus of barking. Mike hopped down from the cab and opened the tailgate.

"Yep, the kites are all in the back here, ready to fly—unless these dumb mutts trampled them to death."

"Can we see them? Where? Which one's mine?"

Mike reached into the back and pulled out a large box kite. "This one is yours, Mickey. I made it myself out of aluminum tubing and parachute cloth."

"Awesome! Thanks, Grandpa!" Mickey grabbed the silver kite from Mike with one hand and pushed his thick blond hair off his forehead with the other. He was a handsome boy of 10, almost as tall as Mike, with the sturdy build of a future football player. With his ragged jeans, bulging pockets, smudged face, and lopsided grin, Mickey had the mischievous look of a modern-day Tom Sawyer, ready for adventure.

Mike punched him playfully. "I just hope I won't need my parachute until after I've sewn up all the holes."

"Where's mine, which one's mine?"

"OK, hang on, Pete. Here, this little jet-propelled number is for you." Peter's blue eyes widened in delight as Mike handed him a sleek, black, delta-wing kite. He grinned, revealing a wide gap where his two front teeth should be. He was a skinny, wiggling six-year-old, with dark hair that hung raggedly over his eyes. He twirled the kite through the air, making airplane sounds. Mike was convinced that Peter could amuse himself for hours in any empty room.

"And last but not least, for Her Majesty . . . this beauty!" He drew out a long, silky, multicolored tube kite and swirled it gracefully around his granddaughter Lori's neck. She was eight and had short-cropped, light brown hair and a sweet, turned up nose, liberally dotted with freckles. As wistful as a wood sprite and as impish as an elf, Lori sprinkled her charm like pixie dust, never failing to capture Mike in her spell.

"Oh, Grandpa! It's beautiful! It's even got purple and pink, my favorite colors!"

"Oooh, purple and pink . . . ," her older brother said, mimicking her. "Gimme a break!"

The front door banged again and Mike's son, Steve, strolled across the lawn, his hands stuffed in the pockets of his cutoffs, his T-shirt hanging out. He had a stocky, muscular build and thinning brown hair. Mike saw himself, 30-some years ago, in his son's energetic stride.

"You coming with us?" Mike asked.

"Naw . . . I promised Cheryl I'd get some stuff done around the house today. Wish I could, though."

"OK then, are you three guys ready to go?" Mike asked.

"Yeah!"

"Well, hop aboard!"

Peter climbed over the tailgate to join Buster and Heinz in the back of the truck, then held up a red, diamond-shaped paper kite with a tail of knotted socks. "Grandpa, who is this kite for?"

"That's my 59 cent special, for a friend of mine. We'll pick her up on our way to the park."

"Her? Is she my age?" Lori asked.

"Nope, she's my age, and she told me she's never flown a kite before. Isn't that awful?"

Steve grinned at him. "Don't tell me you've got a date! Is it that mysterious lady who keeps calling you at the hangar?"

Mike felt his face grow hot. He certainly had no intention of courting Professor Brewster, yet he hadn't been able to stop thinking about her ever since their conversation in the doughnut shop.

"No, it's not like a date or anything. She's awfully

homely, if you want to know the truth, and not my type at all. But she just retired a few months ago, and she doesn't know what to do with herself. I think she's kind of depressed. I feel sorry for her, that's all. I thought maybe we could cheer her up. Put a little fun in her life."

"Sure, Dad . . . whatever you say!" Steve winked at Lori. "Make sure you keep Grandpa out of trouble, all right? See you later."

The kids chattered noisily as Mike drove across town, bragging about the future prospects of their kites and arguing over who would win the contest. Mike drove past the Faith College campus, then turned onto a broad, tree-lined boulevard.

"Wow! Look at the mansions!" Lori said.

Mike slowed down, checking the house numbers until he spotted the right one. He pulled into the long, curving driveway.

"Is this your friend's house, Grandpa? It's big!"

"Yep, this must be it, because there she is."

Wilhelmina knelt in the garden in front of the house, digging tulip bulbs. She wore an old pair of brown tweed slacks, a faded blue windbreaker, and a flowered kerchief on her head. As the truck rattled to a stop, with Buster and Heinz barking loudly in back, she looked up in surprise. Mike jumped down from the cab and waved his cap at her in greeting.

"Hi, Professor. Lovely day, isn't it?"

"Why . . . Mr. Dolan!" She scrambled to her feet, brushing the dirt off her knees.

"My grandkids and I are on our way to a kite flying contest in the park, and I thought maybe you'd like to join us."

"Well . . . thank you, but . . . but I really must finish these bulbs."

Mike grinned and shoved his hands into his pockets. "Now you told me the other day that you never flew a kite when you were a kid and . . . well . . . flying a kite is about the closest you can get to really flying—without leaving the ground, that is. Come on, give it a try."

"No . . . really, I'm not dressed . . ." She flicked an imaginary speck of dirt off her slacks.

Mike guessed from the way she studied the ground that she was trying to think of a tactful excuse. "You look fine to me, Professor. Besides, I've decided not to take 'no' for an answer, so you may as well stop dreaming up excuses and come along."

Her mouth opened and closed soundlessly. She looked like a grounded fish.

"Please? I could really use your help, Ma'am. I've got three kids and three kites, so I'm kind of outnumbered."

He smiled his most charming smile, the one the ladies could never refuse, and she sighed in resignation.

"Oh, all right. Just let me get . . . uh . . . my purse." She disappeared into the house.

Mike untangled kids, kites, and dogs, and settled them down in the back of the truck while he waited.

At last Wilhelmina reappeared, clutching a large, brown leather purse. She had exchanged her windbreaker for a cardigan sweater and removed the kerchief. Mike watched a look of dismay and hesitation cross her face as she approached the battered pickup, as if she hadn't realized when she agreed to come along that she'd have to ride in such a rusted-out hulk.

"It's not too pretty, but it'll get us there."

He took her arm and hoisted her up into the lumpy passenger seat before she could change her mind. Then he ran around to the driver's seat, ground the truck into reverse, and backed out. A few minutes later, Peter popped his head through the rear cab window.

"What's your name?" he asked.

"Professor, I'd like you to meet my grandkids. Peter . . . Mickey . . . and the lovely Princess Lori. This is Professor Brewster, guys."

"Wow! A real professor?" Peter asked.

"Yep, she's the real thing."

The professor sat close to the door, clutching her purse as if afraid it might leap out of her arms. When they pulled into the parking lot, she opened it a crack, peered inside, then closed it again with a loud snap.

Mike tied the dogs to the bumper as the kids scrambled down with their kites. Then he tucked the red paper kite under his arm and helped Wilhelmina from the truck. They walked together to the registration booth where a large banner announced "The Twelfth Annual Kite Flying Contest."

"I want to register four kites," Mike told the girl in the booth.

"Names and ages, please?"

"Mickey Dolan is 10 years old . . . the lovely Princess Lori Dolan is 8 . . . Peter Dolan is 6 . . . and Miss Brewster, here, is 29." The girl glanced up at Wilhelmina and smiled.

"Oh no . . . really, Mr. Dolan," Wilhelmina said. "I'm not going to fly one . . ."

"Sure you are. Come on." He paid the small registration fee, and they hurried to a huge open area of the park. Children and kites of all ages and sizes lined up at one end of the field while a park official, bullhorn in hand, strutted back and forth like a drill sergeant announcing the rules.

"All right, everyone, listen up! Here's how it goes. When the gun goes off, get those kites airborne. In exactly one hour, the whistle will blow and the highest kite wins. Any questions?"

The starting gun boomed, and Mickey took off across the grass as if the officials were shooting at him. The box kite trailed behind him, fighting the forces of gravity.

"That's it, Mickey!" Mike cheered. "Give it more string!"

Mickey unwound his string, watching over his shoulder as he ran. The big kite climbed laboriously, twirling in circles in the breeze. His kite was the first

69

one in the air and the audience applauded.

Peter tugged on his arm. "Will you help me, Grandpa?"

"OK, Pete. Professor, can you help the princess?"

"But . . . but . . . I don't know how!"

"Like this, ladies. Watch." He gave the kite to Pete who ran across the grass with it. Mike fed him the string. As soon as he felt the breeze, Mike yelled, "OK, let it go!" Pete released the kite and it flapped and fluttered noisily above his head. "Like that, girls!"

A moment later, Pete's kite fluttered back to earth like a wounded bird.

While Peter ran to retrieve the kite, Mike coached the professor and Lori. Soon, Lori's kite hovered tentatively in the air above them, then swirled to the ground. "Awww . . . too bad, girls. Try it again."

He turned his attention back to Pete, and after several more tries they finally got the black kite airborne. It fluttered wildly above them. "Grandpa, how's Mickey's doing?"

Mickey had run to the far side of the field and appeared to be doing well. The box kite hung in the air as if pasted to the sky.

"Please help us, Grandpa." Lori was close to tears. Her kite lay in a heap on the grass while the professor crouched beside it, plucking at the tangled mess.

"I'm afraid I'm not much help," Wilhelmina said.

Mike took out his pocket knife, cut off the tangled part, then quickly retied the spool to Lori's kite.

After a minute or two he had it flying in graceful

zigzags above her head, painting swaths of color across the sky like a huge paintbrush. He handed her the string. "It's the most beautiful kite in the whole contest, Princess."

Mike stood for a few minutes with his hands on his hips, gazing at his grandchildren as they flew their kites. When he felt this good it was easy for him to forget that his time was limited, the days left with his grandchildren precious and few. He was alive now, and that was all that mattered. Tomorrow was a long way off.

Finally he picked up the red, diamond-shaped kite with its comical tail of old knotted socks and walked over to Wilhelmina.

"Here you go, Professor. Let's get her up there."

"Oh no . . . really," she said with a frown. "I'd rather just watch."

Mike handed her the spool of kite string, ignoring her protests. "Now, as soon as I let go of the kite give the string a sharp tug, like this. That gives it lift. Then just keep feeding it more string, OK?"

He looked at the profusion of kites dotting the sky, then at his watch. "We'll have to hurry if you're going to win," he said. Before she could reply, Mike raised the kite high above his head and sprinted across the field, his keys and loose change jangling in his pocket. When he felt the kite catch the breeze, he tossed it in the air.

"OK, *now!*" he shouted. She gave a tug and fed out the string exactly as he had shown her, and soon the

71

kite soared above their heads, straining at the string as if longing to climb higher. He sprinted back to Wilhelmina's side shouting, "She wants to sail, Professor! Let it out as fast as you can! That's it! That's it!"

Wilhelmina held the spool loosely, letting the kite take the string, and it climbed quickly to the top of the sky. Her eyes were glued to the kite high above her head, and Mike noticed that the harsh lines of her face seemed to have relaxed from their habitual scowl. She was almost smiling—really smiling—for the first time since he'd met her. When she noticed him staring at her, her cheeks turned red.

"You'd better take it now, Mr. Dolan."

"No way! You're doing great. And please, call me Mike." She glanced at him, then quickly turned her face to the sky, watching the kite soaring high above them.

"Isn't that the greatest feeling in the world, Professor, holding onto that kite? I love the way it kind of pulls at your hands, like it's alive . . . like it wants to pull you up in the air with it . . . almost as if it's saying 'come on, fly with me.' Then your heart just travels right up the string and soars around up there, too, doesn't it? And for a little while you're not bound to the earth any more, but you're tied to the sky! Know what I mean?"

She gave him a peculiar half-smile, then nodded. "Yes, I think maybe I do."

"But you're going to have to give it all the string you

got, if you want to win. I think that orange one and maybe that yellow box kite are higher up than yours. Let out all your string, I'll go check on the kids."

Mike found Lori halfway across the field, in tears. Her line had crossed paths with another kite and now both were grounded, laying under a heap of string, as hopelessly tangled as spaghetti.

He gathered her in his arms and let her bury her face on his shoulder. "Don't cry, Princess . . . don't cry. I know you're disappointed . . . but yours is still the prettiest kite in the whole contest. Come on . . . we'll cut her loose . . . and if you dry those tears I'll take you out for burgers and fries afterward. How about it?"

She wiped her tears and gave him a weak smile.

"That's my girl!" He cut her kite free, then folded it ceremoniously, like a flag at a soldier's funeral. He laid it in her arms.

"There. Now, I wonder where your two brothers are?"

Mike spotted the silver box kite halfway up a tall maple tree at the edge of the field. Mickey was scrambling up the trunk to retrieve it.

"Looks like Mickey got too close to those trees," he said.

Lori pointed to the playground. "And there's Petey." Peter sailed merrily through the air on a swing, the contest forgotten, his kite flapping back and forth a few inches above his head.

"Well, Princess, it looks like the professor is our

only hope for that trophy. Come on, let's go help her out."

They jogged back to Wilhelmina's side, but she seemed oblivious to their presence. She gazed at her kite as if it were a million miles away and her thoughts seemed lost in the clouds above her.

"I think that orange one is still higher than yours, Professor, but if you let out all your string you can probably beat him."

She looked at him in surprise. "Oh, but the string's stretched so tightly already. I'm afraid I'll lose it if I do that. Won't it break?"

"Well, it might. That's a chance you'll have to take. But if you don't take the risk, you're never going to win the contest. May as well go for it. You'll never win by playing it safe, and at least you strike out swinging!"

She looked down at her feet in concentration, as if wrestling with a tremendously important decision. He wanted to remind her that it was only a 59-cent kite, but she seemed so absorbed in thought he didn't want to interrupt.

Finally she relaxed her grip on the spool and cautiously let out more string. But she never took her eyes off the ground, as if afraid to watch the string snap or see her kite sail away into the clouds.

Mike sized up the competition. Only a dozen kites remained in the air and as he watched, Professor Brewster's kite slowly climbed until it was just a red speck, as high as the orange one.

"That's it! Keep going, Professor! You can beat him. We'll tie on some of Lori's string if we have to."

Wilhelmina kept her head lowered, then closed her eyes as she slowly unwound the last of her string.

"Grandpa, she's winning, she's winning! Look!"

"Lori's right! You've got him beat now!"

Wilhelmina finally looked up. "Oh my! I never dreamed it could go so high!"

Suddenly a whistle blew and the crowd let out a cheer.

"You *won!* You *won!*" Lori shouted.

A huge crowd converged on them, complete with reporters, photographers, and even the minicam from a local TV station.

"Can we have your name please, Ma'am?"

"Uh . . . Wilhelmina . . . uh, Brewster . . ."

Flashbulbs popped like fireworks as the contest judge shook her hand and presented her with a small trophy. It stood about eight inches tall, topped with a metallic replica of a kite. Engraved on the base were the words, "12th Annual Kite Flying Contest—1st Place."

"We're going to be on TV!" Lori whispered. Pete and Mickey ran over to join them, kites in hand.

Mike watched in amusement as the reporters peppered Wilhelmina with more questions and congratulations. The attention had flustered her, but she seemed to be enjoying it nonetheless. He was glad he'd brought her. At last the excitement began to die down.

"So, you're going to be in the news," Mike said, patting her shoulder. "Aren't you glad you took that chance?"

She smiled slightly and nodded. "I wish I could see Dean Bradford's face when he reads about it in the newspaper."

"Yep, I'd say you did pretty good for your first time flying, Professor."

Her smile vanished. "Please don't call me that, Mike. It's Wilhelmina."

"OK, Willymina. But now I think you'd better start reeling it in. It's probably going to take awhile."

She stared up at the kite, soaring high above them and sighed. "Yes, you're right. Though it seems a shame . . ." She began to turn the spool between her hands, slowly reeling in the taut string. Suddenly there was a twanging sound, as if someone had plucked a violin, and the string went slack in her hand. The red kite soared out of sight.

"It broke!" she cried. "I'm sorry . . . I lost your kite."

"Oh, hey, that's all right. At least you won the contest before it broke. And it seems kind of fitting, don't you think? Almost like you set it free."

Wilhelmina nodded thoughtfully. "I could tell by the way it tugged in my hands that it wanted to go forever."

"Can't we get it back, Grandpa?" Pete asked. "That was the best kite!"

Mike scooped him up in his arms as they walked toward the truck. "Tell you what, Pete. You and me and the professor will go up in the Cessna and we'll fly all over the city until we see that kite roaming around up there. Then you can open the window, reach out, and grab it!" Mike tickled Peter until he giggled helplessly.

When they reached the truck, Buster and Heinz greeted them with tail-wagging enthusiasm. "Can I ride up front, Grandpa?" Lori asked.

"Sure thing, Princess." He tossed her up in the cab and helped Wilhelmina in beside her.

A few minutes after they were underway, Lori turned to Wilhelmina. "Are you going to be our new grandma?"

"Lori!" Mike sputtered for something to say. He was too embarrassed to think. Peter stuck his head through the open window of the cab.

"Well, we only got one grandma, you know. And she lives in Texas. We like the professor 'cause she flies kites."

"Uh . . . yeah . . . she's great at flying kites," Mike mumbled. He glanced at Wilhelmina and saw her studying the trophy in her lap, her cheeks burning. He stepped on the accelerator. "Sorry, Professor . . . these kids have no manners at all."

It was only a few blocks to the fast-food restaurant, but it seemed much farther to Mike. Maybe if he stuffed enough French fries in their mouths they wouldn't be able to talk, let alone embarrass him again. When he pulled the truck into the parking lot, the kids cheered.

"OK, everybody out. We're going to celebrate this victory in style."

He seated them at a table and returned a few minutes later with a tray full of burgers and fries. "Here you go, Willymina, one jumbo burger with onions and fries."

She moaned, clutching her hand to her side. "Oh my! I can't . . ."

"Sure you can." He lifted his Styrofoam coffee cup in salute. "Cheers! To the greatest kite-flyer in town, Willymina Brewster!"

The kids put their hamburgers down long enough to applaud. Wilhelmina managed a smile.

It was almost dark when Mike finally pulled his pickup into Wilhelmina's driveway. He helped her out of the cab and walked her to her door.

"Thanks for coming with us. I hope you had fun."

"Yes, I did! Thank you, Mr. . . . I mean, Mike. Oh, and here's your trophy." He backed toward the truck, holding his hands up in protest.

"No way! You won that trophy fair and square. It's yours, Professor. Put it with all your music trophies." He climbed in and started the engine, then ground the gears into reverse. He had started to back up when he thought he heard Wilhelmina shouting.

"Mr. Dolan! Stop! Wait a minute! Please!" She charged down the driveway toward him, rummaging for something in her purse at the same time. "Wait! I want to give you something . . ."

"No way, Professor! I don't want any money!"

"But . . . but . . ."

"You don't owe me a thing," he said, leaning out the open window. "Today was my treat. See you!"

Ignoring her frantic protests, Mike swung the truck out onto the boulevard and drove away.

The following day Wilhelmina was late for church. Her gall bladder had waged war against the French fries all night, and she had slept poorly. When the alarm sounded she barely managed to drag herself out of bed and get dressed. Where would she find the strength to play the organ?

When she stopped by Carol's house to pick her up, she found her already waiting beside the curb. Wilhelmina braced herself for a scolding, but Carol got into the car without a word.

"Good morning, Carol . . . sorry I'm late." She didn't reply. Instead, Carol peered at her strangely, as if Wilhelmina still wore curlers in her hair. Wilhelmina checked her reflection in the rearview mirror.

"What's the matter with you," she said crossly. "Why are you looking at me that way?"

"I just can't believe it!" Carol said. "I turned on the news last night and there you were! Flying a *kite,* of all things!"

"Oh, come on, Carol. I was on the news. So what?"

"But I couldn't believe my eyes! We've been friends for ages and ages, and I've never known you to fly a *kite* before!"

"You make it sound like I committed murder."

"Well, good heavens, Wilhelmina! It's supposed to be for kids! Whatever possessed you to enter a *kite* contest?"

Mike Dolan. He was the cause of all this. Wilhelmina recalled how he had driven off without the tracts again, and her irritation turned to anger.

"I had a very good reason for going to the park, and I accidentally won the contest. That's all. I hardly plan to make a career of it. Now can we drop it?"

"OK, but . . ." Carol was still staring at her.

"But what!"

"It's just so unlike you, Wilhelmina. And you've never been late picking me up before. Are you sure you're all right?"

"Well, I'm not becoming senile, if that's what you're thinking. I went to the park to help someone—"

"Who?"

"Never mind. I didn't intend to get involved in the contest, believe me. But now I'm glad that I did. It was fun." She was surprised by her own confession.

They rode in silence the rest of the way to church with Carol stealing glances at her from time to time. Wilhelmina left Carol in the church lobby and hurried up to the choir room, already several minutes late for the preservice rehearsal. The choir members were dressed in their robes and listening to the music director, a former colleague of hers from the college. She tried to sneak in unnoticed, but as she opened the door the director stopped midsentence. All eyes were immediately upon her.

"Ah, there you are, Professor Brewster. I was just sharing the news of your new retirement career with the choir."

The director unfolded the morning newspaper and held up a photo spread of the kite-flying contest. The disbelieving stares of 42 choir members bored through Wilhelmina. She may as well have been arrested for running naked through the park. The director tacked the article to the bulletin board for everyone to see.

"First place, Professor! Good show! Would you like to share the secret of your great success with us?"

She heard titters of laughter and the lead tenor, also a former colleague, covered his mouth to hide a smirk. Wilhelmina wished she had never agreed to go with Mike Dolan.

"I'd really rather not talk about it," she said.

"Oh, I see. You can't divulge any secrets of the kite-flying profession, right?" The choir roared with laughter.

Wilhelmina had never felt so mortified in her life. Her colleagues usually held her in high esteem, applauding her achievements, not laughing at them. The insinuation that flying a kite was her new retirement career hurt the most. She seated herself at the practice piano with the remnants of her dignity and refused to acknowledge the director's cruel jibes.

Later, as the choir filed into the sanctuary for the service, Wilhelmina overheard their whispered comments: "Who would have ever guessed! . . . so unlike her! . . . Can you imagine?" She longed to escape the mocking stares and snickers.

The church service was disastrous. Wilhelmina played the organ prelude so rapidly that Pastor Stockman barely had time to take his seat on the platform before leaping up to the pulpit. She rushed both hymns, leaving the congregation gasping for breath, and took the tempo much too fast on the choir anthem. The director waved his arms frantically at her, trying to slow the stampede. Through it all, Wilhelmina thought of Mike Dolan. This was his fault. She relived her undignified sprint down the driveway, waving the tracts at him like a crazed woman, and closed her eyes in shame.

Why was God subjecting her to this public humiliation? She was only trying to do what He commanded. Would He make her suffer more degradation, like the 10 plagues of Egypt, before finally delivering Mr. Dolan's eternal soul to the Promised Land?

She stomped the organ pedals during the closing hymn as if they were responsible for her disgrace.

Rescue the perishing, care for the dying,
Snatch them in pity from sin and the grave . . .

How was she supposed to do that? Every time she came up with a plan things seemed to go all wrong. She pulled out most of the organ stops as she launched into the final verse until even the stained-glass windows rattled:

Rescue the perishing, duty demands it,
Strength for thy labor the Lord will provide . . .

What about public humiliation? Was there a verse about that?

By the time the hymn ended, Wilhelmina had managed to drown out the choir entirely. The director was quivering. Wilhelmina didn't care.

When she finished her organ postlude and the sanctuary had emptied, she decided not to return to the choir room to face more snickers and stares. She was attempting to sneak out through a side door to the parking lot when she ran into Pastor Stockman, waving the newspaper article. Wilhelmina groaned.

"Well, well, well, Miss Brewster! What a surprise to see you in the news. I knew you were a woman of many talents but I had no idea you were a champion kite flyer too."

"Yes . . . well . . . I . . ."

"I'm so glad to see you're enjoying your retirement years." He beamed at her and patted her arm as if she were a child, then hurried away.

The irony of his final comment shattered her. She fought back her tears. She wasn't enjoying her retirement. Her life was empty and lonely beyond words. She had found a few minutes of pleasure in the simple act of flying a kite, a few minutes where she could forget her boring existence, and everyone treated it like a farce, as if she had chosen it as a career to replace teaching. Why did everyone see it as a big joke instead of what it really was—a tragic commentary on the senselessness of forced retirement?

Wilhelmina waited in the car for Carol. She was

always one of the last people to leave the church for fear she'd miss a juicy tidbit of gossip. When she finally arrived, Carol babbled for several minutes about the Powers' new baby and the Baldwins' oldest son before finally coming to the biggest news item.

". . . But *you* were really the main topic of discussion today, dear. You and your *kite* contest."

"Why is everyone making such a big deal out of nothing?" Wilhelmina said wearily. "I don't understand it."

"Well, Wilhelmina, it's so unlike you!"

"If I hear that one more time, I'll scream."

"Well, if you didn't want to bear the brunt of everyone's gossip, you never should have done such a thing."

"Since when is it a crime to fly a kite!"

"I didn't say it was, but at our age . . . you know . . ." Carol left the sentence dangling ungraciously.

Wilhelmina gripped the steering wheel tighter as she drove, struggling to control her anger. But Carol didn't speak again until they reached her house.

"Thanks for the ride . . . and try to get some rest, dear, you haven't been yourself lately." Carol was about to close the door when Wilhelmina called her back.

"Carol . . . I want you to know that flying that kite was fun. I'm not sorry I did it, even at my age." Carol rolled her eyes and quickly slammed the door, as if Wilhelmina's insanity might be contagious.

When Wilhelmina got home her house seemed cold and very, very large—larger than it ever had before. She spotted the trophy on the kitchen table where she had left it the night before, and she picked it up, remembering the tug of the kite in her hands as it pulled, straining to be free. Mr. Dolan had been right—her heart had soared with it. And for just a little while she, too, had flown far above the earth, tied to the sky.

It had been such innocent fun, such a simple, ordinary act. Why had everyone laughed at her? Her colleagues had gazed at her with shocked surprise, as if she had done something completely out of character. Was her life so predictable, so dull, that the ordinary act of flying a kite seemed extraordinary when she did it? Suddenly, in their reactions, she saw herself as she really was. Wilhelmina Brewster was not someone who had fun.

"I'm an old stuffed shirt," she said aloud, and though she wished it weren't true, she knew that it was. Anyone acquainted with Mike Dolan wouldn't have been surprised to learn he had won the contest. Mike enjoyed life to the fullest, what little of it was left for him.

She recalled her failed efforts to give him the tracts, picturing the somber cover that promised hell-fire to the unbeliever. Then she saw herself—Wilhelmina the pompous stuffed shirt—coldly handing it to kind, smiling, dying Mr. Dolan. She grabbed her purse and yanked out both tracts, then tore them into tiny shreds, not even caring that the pieces scattered all over her kitchen floor like confetti.

"O dear Lord," she whispered, "I don't want to be this way!"

When had she stopped having fun? Or had she ever begun? Her entire life had been rigidly disciplined and structured around a sense of duty, leaving no room for spontaneity. Wilhelmina picked up the trophy again, the only prize she had ever won for something other than music, and walked into the living room with it, carrying it like a sacred object. She cleared a space in the center of the mantelpiece, pushing aside her grandmother's antique marble clock, and set the gaudy trophy in its place. She stepped back to look, smiling faintly through her tears.

5

Friday, September 25, 1987

Wilhelmina rang her brother's doorbell and waited. The drive down to New Haven had seemed longer than usual, but an evening spent with her dynamic younger brother would more than compensate for the tiring trip. She'd come with the hope that Peter could offer her some sound advice for the problem that she'd carried in her heart all week—Mike Dolan.

Peter flung the door open with customary exuberance, taking both her hands in his. "Mina! It's wonderful to see you! Come in, come in!" He smiled his broad, warm smile that reminded Wilhelmina so much of their mother. Peter strongly resembled the Scandinavian side of the family, Mother's side, with his fair skin and ruddy blond hair and beard. His smile, with the tiny space between his two front teeth, was Mother's smile, soothing and warm. Wilhelmina had inherited their father's stern, Puritanical, New England features.

The moment she stepped into the apartment the savory aroma of her sister-in-law's cooking made Wilhelmina's mouth water. As they talked about the weather and the traffic in New Haven, Wilhelmina's eyes feasted on the exquisitely decorated rooms. Peter was headmaster of an undergraduate residential college at Yale, a sophisticated version of dormitory parents. His spacious apartment was comfortably integrated into the Old World architecture of the university, with tall, arched windows of leaded glass; broad, golden oak woodwork; a white fireplace of imported Italian marble. It wasn't the sort of apartment you would trust to amateur tastes, so Peter had hired a professional decorator, who had achieved the desired effect with lots of original artwork and European antiques.

Peter's wife, Janice, floated in from the kitchen and brushed Wilhelmina's cheek with her lips. Her bangles and bracelets tinkled faintly as she moved.

"How are you, dear? We're so glad you decided to come down." She was slim and very fashionable, a woman Peter could proudly display on his arm at faculty parties, a sensational hostess, and an expert at university politics.

They all moved into the elegant dining room for what Janice had insisted would be just potluck. But Janice's idea of potluck was crab in clamshells, fresh cream of asparagus soup, watercress and endive salad, and ragout of pork with chestnuts.

As they dined, Peter talked about his latest crop of scholars and his schedule of courses, while Janice brought Wilhelmina up to date on their two children and five grandchildren. When they'd finished their cheesecake, they took their coffee into Peter's study.

It was a comfortable man's room with warm walnut paneling and deep leather sofas and chairs. A massive bank of shelves, tightly packed with books, dominated one wall. Peter's antique desk was barely visible beneath mounds of paper and a sprawling computer.

"This is the only room in which Jan lets me indulge my fondness for an after-dinner pipe," Peter said. He sank into his favorite armchair and began fiddling with his tobacco and pipe tools. He usually spent more time playing with the pipe than actually smoking it, and Wilhelmina suspected that Peter performed these rituals because it suited his image as a professor rather than from any dependence on nicotine.

"So, how's everything at dear old Faith College?" he asked when his pipe was finally functioning.

Wilhelmina stared at him. "Peter, you know that I'm retired now."

"Well, not altogether, are you? I thought you were only slowing down to part-time."

"I thought so, too, but it didn't happen that way." She hoped her voice wouldn't break and betray her. "I moved out of my office last spring, and that's the last I've heard from anybody."

Peter nearly dropped his pipe. "What!"

"Well, they do send my pension checks every month."

"What's going on up there?" he asked sternly, as he got up from his overstuffed chair. "I'll give Dean Bradford a call right now."

"No, Peter! That's not necessary."

"The Brewster family helped make that college what it is today. They can't just throw you out like that!"

"Peter, listen to me. How could I face everyone if I had to claim family privilege to beg for my job?"

"But they have no right—"

"I know, I know. I was angry, too, at first. But it's OK now. Really. I'm retired, and I have other things to do."

"Anyone for more coffee?" Janice hated any kind of conflict, real or imagined, and Wilhelmina knew from the faint tinkling sound that she was wringing her hands. Peter waved her away.

"Listen, I know you, Mina. This job was your life. You can't lose your career overnight and tell me it's all right, that you've found something else to do. What else *is* there for you to do?"

The truth hurt. Tears sprang to Wilhelmina's eyes. She was furious with herself for revealing her weakness to her brother, for tarnishing the image he had of her as a strong, independent woman.

"Just forget it, OK, Peter?"

"All right. I'm sorry, Mina. I didn't mean to upset you."

"Promise me you'll stay out of it."

"If that's what you want." He sighed and sank down in his chair. "Anyway, I should talk. My time is coming, too, in another three years."

"What will you do?" Wilhelmina was grateful to shift the spotlight off herself.

Peter motioned to the overloaded shelves behind him. "I'll be busy for 20 years trying to read all the books I want to read. And there are at least eight or nine books rattling around in my head that I want to write. An editor friend from Yale Press is nagging me to write one of them this summer."

"We want to spend more time with the children too," Janice added. She appeared relieved to return to a neutral subject. "And our grandchildren, of course. How's your work for the Cancer Society going? Are you still involved with them?"

"I'm on their board of directors this year. And my friend, Carol, talked me into doing volunteer work with the Hospice Association this fall. Which brings me to one of the reasons I wanted to talk to you, Peter."

"Oh? What's that?" He sat forward attentively,

puffing little clouds of aromatic smoke.

"Well, one of the terminal patients I met confided that he's not going to wait for cancer to kill him. He plans to kill himself." Janice gasped. "I don't know . . . what do you think, Peter? Is that so wrong?"

"From a Christian perspective? Yes, of course. Absolutely."

"That's what I thought, too, at first. But lately I'm not so sure. He said that if he's going to die anyway, what difference does it make when or how? He's trying to spare his family a lot of pain. You know what a long, horrible death cancer can be. Remember how much Mother suffered . . . and how hard it was for us to watch her die like that? He's got three little grandchildren who love him dearly. Is it wrong to want to shield them from his suffering?"

"I'll get more coffee." Janice slipped from the room, her bracelets tinkling delicately.

"Are you certain he isn't trying to spare himself the pain and not just his family?" Peter asked. "Maybe he's looking for the easy way out."

"I can't blame him for wanting that, can you? People say suicide is the coward's choice, but I think it would take a good deal of courage to steer your airplane into a mountain."

"Is that what he's planning to do?"

"Something like that."

Peter sighed and laid down his pipe. "The Bible says that there is a season for everything, a time to be born and a time to die. It's not up to us to choose the time or the manner in which we die. That decision belongs to God. Our Christian heritage teaches that suicide is wrong, under any circumstances. Christians sometimes get confused, however, because the Bible also says in Philippians that death is gain for a believer, and to be with Christ is better by far. We're taught to look forward to it."

"Well, that's another problem. He isn't a Christian."

"Then he's not going to escape any pain by killing himself . . ." Peter hesitated. "But where do you come into the picture, Mina? I thought your involvement with the Cancer Society was on an administrative level. I didn't realize you would actually have personal contact with patients."

Something about Peter's attitude stung Wilhelmina. His tone was disparaging, as if working with patients on a personal level was extremely distasteful. She recognized it as an attitude she had shared until recently. Until Mike Dolan.

"I don't know how I got involved, but I am. He's a very nice person, but he isn't a Christian. I'd like to talk to him about God, but I don't know where to start. That's a terrible confession, coming from someone who's been a Christian nearly all her life, but it's true. I was hoping you could help me. How do you convince someone to believe in the existence of God?"

"Ah! Christian apologetics! It's one of my favorite subjects." As he switched into his role as professor,

92

Peter couldn't stay seated. He rose solemnly from his seat and soon lost himself in his subject as he began to lecture.

"The arguments for the existence of God can be grouped into three main categories. First, the belief in the existence of God is intuitive; both necessary and universal. And according to Kant those are the infallible tests for distinguishing pure from empirical knowledge. That it is universal is shown by the fact that even primitive cultures espouse some beliefs in a supreme being or beings, albeit primitive ones. And it is necessary in that to deny the existence of God is to do grave injustice to the laws of our own nature."

Peter was in great form now, and he paced back and forth across the room expostulating as if he had a lecture hall full of freshmen; sometimes clasping his hands behind his back as he talked, sometimes pressing his fingertips together in front of him, sometimes gesturing broadly.

"Second, the existence of God is assumed by the Holy Scriptures to be true. Nowhere in the Bible will you find scholarly dissertations arguing the existence of a Divine Being. Rather, His existence is presupposed, and the Scriptures record the general and special revelations of that God to man."

He paused, as if to give Wilhelmina time to write everything down in her notebook. His years of teaching had given him a rhythm suited to the writing speed of his students.

"Third, the belief in the existence of God can be corroborated by rational arguments. Mind you, these don't constitute proofs of an empirical nature because God, being a spirit, cannot be subjected to proof as can the material world. However, there are five rational arguments, and the cumulative weight of these is sufficient to sustain belief."

As Wilhelmina listened she found herself thinking of her father. Of the three Brewster children, Peter was the most like Father. Not in appearance, but in his facility for clear, logical thinking and in his brilliant intellect. Father loved all three of his children, of course, but he was probably proudest of Peter—a tenured professor of religious studies at Yale with a Ph.D. in both philosophy and religion.

"The cosmological argument proceeds from the supposition of cause; everything begun must have an adequate cause. That the universe was begun necessarily leads to the conclusion that it therefore must have an adequate cause for its creation."

So much of what Peter was saying seemed vaguely familiar to Wilhelmina. How many times throughout the years had she seen Father pacing just like this and expostulating the arguments for the existence of God for his seminary students. How she loved her father! It wasn't the warm, openly affectionate way Mike's grandchildren loved him; Father was almost a God-figure to her, someone she held in awesome respect and obeyed for fear of losing his approval. He demanded a lot from his children, but he always acknowledged their achievements with recognition and praise.

"Then there is the teleological argument, which is the argument from design, recognizing the order and intelligent purpose in the universe."

Wilhelmina could hardly bring herself to visit her father in the nursing home anymore. He was 89, and his last stroke had taken away any remaining resemblance to the father she loved and remembered. He was partially paralyzed, nearly blind, and incapable of caring for any of his own basic needs. The brilliant mind she had loved and admired was lost, locked away from her by the breakdown of blood vessels and nerves. Sometimes he knew who she was when she visited, but most of the time she was a stranger to him and he to her. His body was kept alive by the wonders of medicine, but the person, the spirit of her father, was lost to her forever. It was the same dilemma that Mike faced—why strive to prolong a life that is really a living death?

"Then there is the ontological argument, which states that the very idea of God is the proof of His existence and—"

"Peter."

"Huh . . . ?" He looked at her in surprise, almost as if he had forgotten that anyone was listening to him.

"I'm sorry to interrupt, but I'll never remember all this. Is there much more?"

"Well, there's still the moral argument and the argument from congruity. But I can give you some books that explain all of this, and you can sort it out on your own."

He strode over to the study shelves and pulled off several large volumes of leather-bound books. "Here's some lectures on systematic theology and a couple of Christian apologetics . . . and I'll throw in some Kant and Hume just to round things off." He built an impressive stack of books on the floor in front of her.

"I really appreciate it, Peter."

"No problem." He dropped into his armchair and returned to his neglected pipe.

"Have you been up to see Father lately?" Wilhelmina asked.

"You know, I've been meaning to go, but I just can't seem to get away."

"We send him little cards now and then," Janice said. She had returned to the room with fresh coffee in the middle of Peter's lecture. "And a fresh flower arrangement every week or so to cheer him up."

"I've been teaching an honors tutorial on philosophical and Christian ethics, and it has really kept me tied down." Peter's eyes avoided Wilhelmina's as he scooped more tobacco into his pipe and tamped it down. "How is Father?"

"About the same. Maybe a little worse. The doctor says his heart is all right but his mind . . . well, he's in another world most of the time. Very confused." There was an awkward silence. "Do you think he'd want to go on living like this if he could choose?" Wilhelmina asked quietly. "Would he want to be kept alive indefinitely, robbed of his mind and his dignity?"

"Now you're back to the same question we were discussing earlier and your friend with the airplane. Again, our faith teaches that it's wrong to take life and death into our own hands."

"But is it wrong to refuse medical intervention if it's simply prolonging our existence, not curing us? What's the next step for Father . . . intravenous feedings, respirators, pacemakers, miracle drugs? They might keep his body going, but Father is already gone, Peter. He's lost to us. Maybe God is saying, 'Let him die,' and we're taking death into our own hands by keeping him alive."

"We've got to make a clear distinction between prolonging life and facilitating death. It's wrong to speed up the process of death just to relieve suffering or for the family's convenience or because the medical insurance has run out. But that's quite different from refusing artificial life support in patients for whom death is imminent and unavoidable. According to Ecclesiastes, God has appointed a time for Father to die. We can't hasten that process just because we don't think Father's present existence is worth prolonging."

"Do we have to talk about such grim subjects?" Janice asked. "Come on, we don't see Wilhelmina very often. Let's not spoil such a nice visit."

"You're right, darling," Peter said. "What do you feel like doing tonight, Mina? There's a Yale symphony concert, I think. Janice, why don't you call the box office at Woolsey Hall and see if they still have tickets?"

"Oh, please don't bother," Wilhelmina said. "You don't need to take me anywhere. I'm not sure I feel like a concert."

Janice paid no attention. Her bracelets jingled as she dialed the number. Peter evidently didn't hear her either. He rooted through his desk drawer mumbling, "I thought I had the concert schedule in here someplace . . . Ah! Here it is. Let's see . . . tonight they're doing Beethoven's Ninth with the university choir and soloists. You should enjoy that, Mina."

"They still have tickets," Janice said. "Shall I reserve three?"

Wilhelmina did not want to go. She used to feel challenged and stimulated by a good performance, but now that music was no longer a part of her life, there seemed little point in listening to it. The concert would only rekindle painful memories and remind her of her loss.

Peter was watching her closely, waving the concert schedule in front of her. Janice held one hand over the telephone receiver, waiting. Wilhelmina sighed.

"I guess we could go, if you both want to."

"Great! Jan, tell them to reserve three seats on the main floor. And maybe we can stop somewhere for coffee and a bite afterward."

Peter would pick someplace very elegant and expensive. Wilhelmina remembered the coffee she had shared with Mike in the smoky, little doughnut shop, and she wondered if her brother's teleological and ontological arguments for the existence of God were really what Mike needed. Perhaps Father would have known what to say to Mike and how to say it, but Father couldn't help her anymore.

"We should walk over," Peter said. "It's a gorgeous evening." He pulled their jackets out of the front closet and steered everyone out the door. But Wilhelmina's heart felt leaden and weary as she walked across the starlit campus.

Wilhelmina sat in her car in the parking lot of the nursing home for several minutes, steeling herself. Visiting Father, witnessing his helplessness and loss of dignity, always depressed her. No wonder Peter and Janice avoided it.

Inside, the lounge of the church-sponsored home was cheerful and pleasant, tastefully decorated to resemble a family living room. But the lingering odor of disinfectant and the flower arrangements from recent funerals spoiled the illusion. Today was visiting day, and nearly all the sofas and chairs were filled with people, chatting happily with their families and friends. These were the elderly who lived in the seniors' complex in the east wing. Father lived in the west wing. The atmosphere in the personal care complex wasn't nearly as cheerful.

Wilhelmina stopped at the nurses' station to talk to the head nurse. "Good afternoon. I was wondering how my father is doing?"

"About the same as when you visited last week, Professor Brewster. He's still having trouble sleeping at night. The doctor will be adjusting his medication."

"Has he been eating?"

"Well, his appetite has never been very good, as you know—" A chilling cry from one of the rooms interrupted her. "Will you excuse me for a minute, please?" The nurse hurried down the polished hallway, her shoes squeaking slightly.

The mournful shrieks followed Wilhelmina down the corridor to her father's room. The smell of disinfectant and urine was overpowering. She hated the thought of leaving her father in a place like this, but there was no other choice.

He sat slumped in his wheelchair, as usual, staring vacantly. How he would hate for anyone to see him like this—shriveled and weary, his face unshaved, his hair greasy and uncombed. He was loosely tied with restraints as if they expected him to suddenly decide he had better things to do and to rise from his chair and leave. She untied him as she bent to kiss his cheek.

"Hello, Father. It's me . . . Wilhelmina."

He looked up, but there was no light in his eyes, no sign that he recognized her. She could have been one of the nurses or a perfect stranger. She took his hand in both of hers, stroking it gently, talking quietly to him for several minutes until she finally ran out of things to say.

The top of his dresser was covered with flower arrangements in various stages of demise, and cheerful get-well cards were stuck in the crack around his mirror. Did he even see them? Did he know who they were from? Why did she bother to come? Was it for her father's sake or for her own?

"Father . . . do you know who I am?" she asked. He didn't respond. Suddenly it became very important to Wilhelmina that he recognize her, that she receive some sign that this shell of a man was really her father, the man she loved so deeply.

"Let's go for a walk," she said. Ignoring the rules and regulations, she wheeled her father down the hall, out of the personal care wing with its shrieks and foul smells. She wanted to pretend, however briefly, that he was himself again, that they were visiting together like the dozens of other senior citizens and their families.

The hallway and nurses' station were deserted. No one challenged her as she wheeled him into the lounge. All the sofas and chairs were occupied, so she pushed him over to the piano and sat down on the bench.

"Shall I play for you, Father?" He seemed to be a little more alert, stimulated by the movement and chatter of people all around him. She began to play, very softly at first. But soon she forgot where she was, playing louder, stronger, as the music transported her. Beethoven. Chopin. Liszt. She never noticed that the conversations had stopped or that everyone was listening to her. Nor did she notice that her father had closed his eyes and that a single tear rolled silently down his cheek.

When she finally ran out of music, the spontaneous applause startled her. She nodded slightly in acknowledgment. Then Wilhelmina raised her hands to the keyboard again. Softly, almost like a lullaby, she played her father's favorite hymn, "Abide with Me." The words drifted through her mind as she played:

Swift to its close ebbs out life's little day.
Earth's joys grow dim; its glories pass away;
Change and decay in all around I see;
O Thou who changest not, abide with me.

She had spoken to her father without words, telling him all that her heart longed to say, reaching out to touch him through her music. She closed the lid to the keyboard and rose to take him back to his room. But he was looking at her intently, moving his mouth as if struggling to speak. She knelt beside him and took his hand. His voice was barely a whisper.

"My Mina . . ."

6

Saturday, October 3, 1987

Mike knocked on his son's screen door, then let himself in. "Anybody home?"

"Come on in, Dad," Cheryl called from the kitchen. "Dinner's almost ready. Steve ran down to the store for some more beer. He'll be back in a minute."

The modest, three-bedroom house had a comfortable, lived-in look with worn carpeting and plaid slipcovers on the furniture. Mike kicked off his work boots and made himself at home.

G.I. Joe and his troops had their headquarters under the coffee table with Mickey as their commander-in-chief. Peter, dressed in army fatigues, helped Luke Skywalker command the rebel forces from their base beside the TV.

"Hey, this place looks like occupied France during World War II," Mike said. He carefully threaded his way through the battle zone in his stocking feet. He knew from experience the pain of stepping on a dead soldier or discarded weapon lying hidden in the gold shag carpet.

A row of assorted dolls, bears, and other creatures watched the battle from the sofa, where Lori served tea. She offered Mike a tiny cup and saucer.

"Want some tea, Grandpa?"

"I'd love some." He slurped the pretend tea noisily. "Say, who's winning the war down there?"

"I am," Mickey said. "I have a better air force."

"You do not!" Pete shouted. "I have the Millennium Falcon!"

The battle raged fiercely for several minutes, with missiles flying and bombs exploding, until Steve came in with a six-pack under his arm.

"Supper's ready," Cheryl called from the kitchen.

Everyone took their places around the crowded dining room table. The heavy, greasy smell of fried chicken filled the air. Mike usually loved the smell, but tonight, for some reason, he didn't find it appealing. His stomach felt queasy, and he hoped he could manage to eat at least some of Cheryl's dinner so he wouldn't insult her. He took only a small portion of mashed potatoes and peas, then chose a small drumstick from the platter of chicken.

"Come on, Dad, you're allowed more than one piece of chicken around here. Take some more." Steve held the platter out to him.

"This is plenty for now."

"You're getting downright thin, you know it? Don't you think you're carrying this diet business a little too far?"

"You're just jealous. Look at the beer belly on you."

Steve patted his T-shirt where it bulged out above his belt. "Yeah, I know, I know. But I really don't think you should try to lose any more weight, Dad. You don't look so good."

"Just saving room for dessert. I've got my eye on that apple pie over there."

Mike felt worse by the minute. He toyed with his food without eating much, but everyone was too busy with his own plate to notice.

"Mom, Petey's taking all the gravy," Lori said.

"Peter, no more until you finish your peas."

"Isn't there any more white meat?" Mickey asked. "I hate dark meat."

"Quit complaining and eat what's already on your plate." Steve stood and walked out to the refrigerator. "Want a beer, Dad?"

Mike's stomach did a quick flop, as if he'd hit an updraft. "No thanks, I'll pass." He picked up his drumstick, but just as it reached his mouth a wave of nausea hit him and he knew he was going to be sick. He pushed his chair away from the table and bolted for the bathroom.

Afterward he felt weak and shaky. He shoved aside the shampoo bottles and toy boats and sat on the edge of the bathtub with his head down, hoping the dizziness would pass. He was angry at himself for having to leave the table. Steve would probably start asking questions again. A moment later someone knocked on the bathroom door.

"Dad? Are you all right?"

"Yeah, Steve. I'm fine. Go finish your dinner. I'll be there in a minute."

Steve opened the door. "You're not all right. Look at you! You're all green around the gills. What's going

105

on, Dad? Level with me, will you?"

"Just a touch of the flu, I guess."

"That's what you said the other day at the hangar when the same thing happened."

"Yeah, well, it's probably something going around. Either that or I'm poisoning myself with my own cooking. My dogs eat the leftovers, and they haven't been feeling too great either." He tried to chuckle, but he saw by Steve's frown that he wasn't buying the story.

"Have you seen the doctor for a checkup lately?"

"What is this, the third degree? As a matter of fact, I have been to the doctor's. Couple of weeks ago." He hoped this news would pacify Steve.

"And . . . ?"

". . . And what?"

"Do I have to drag it out of you? What did he say?"

Mike didn't want to lie to his son, but he didn't want to tell him the truth either. "Well, I'm still here, aren't I? You know how doctors are. He'd have slapped me in the hospital by now if I wasn't A-OK. Now come on, let's get out of here."

Steve didn't move. "Are you sure you checked out all right?"

"You're worse than an old lady, Steve. Call Dr. Bennett yourself if you don't believe me." He hoped Steve wouldn't call his bluff.

"I can get someone else to fly that charter for you tomorrow if you're not up to it."

"No way! I'll be fine tomorrow. Go finish your dinner."

Steve studied him for a moment then reluctantly returned to the table. The house seemed to sway as Mike followed him. He wouldn't be able to finish his food or force down any apple pie either.

"I'm really sorry, Cheryl," he said. "Your dinner was great, but I seem to have caught some kind of flu bug. I hope you'll excuse me."

"That's OK, Dad. Why don't you lie down for a while?"

"We don't have to go out tonight if you don't feel up to babysitting," Steve said.

"I'll be fine. The kids can take care of me for a change."

Mike eased into Steve's recliner, slowly tilting it back as far as it would go. He wouldn't be able to keep up this facade much longer. Steve was already suspicious. The longer Mike delayed, the greater the likelihood that Steve would learn the truth and ground him permanently. Mike closed his eyes, feeling very drowsy all of a sudden. Soft, gray clouds of sleep closed in around him. He would have to take his final flight very soon.

When Mike awoke, he couldn't tell if he'd slept several hours or a few minutes. Then he heard the clatter of dishes and Lori and Mickey arguing over whose turn it was to clear the table, and he knew it had been a short nap. His stomach had settled, and he no longer felt like he was flying through heavy turbulence. He pushed the recliner to a sitting position and picked up the evening paper, hoping to appear fully recovered for his son's benefit. A moment later Steve and Cheryl walked into the living room dressed to go out.

"How are you feeling, Dad?" she asked.

"I'm fine now. This is the weirdest flu I ever had. One minute I feel fine and the next . . . whew! But I'm on the upswing now. I just hope none of you catch it."

Steve studied him for a long moment as if trying to see what was going on inside him. Mike flipped through the newspaper with apparent unconcern. Finally, Steve let out a long sigh.

"All right, I guess we'll get going. Hey, you kids, Mom and I are leaving. You behave yourselves and don't give Grandpa a hard time."

Mike turned to the sports pages to check the latest major league standings, ignoring Lori's periodic announcements of who was helping and who wasn't. The squabbles continued until eventually the supper dishes got loaded into the dishwasher and the kids wandered into the living room.

"Are you still sick, Grandpa?" Lori slipped her slender arm around Mike's neck. He tossed the newspaper onto the floor and pulled her on his knee.

"No, I'm much better now, Princess."

"Will you tell us a story?" Peter asked, crawling onto Mike's other knee. Mike savored the warmth and vitality of their sweaty bodies and the way they seemed to melt into his arms.

"Oh, what a lapful I've got! Aren't you guys ever going to stop growing? I can hardly hold you both anymore."

"Tell us a story about flying," Mickey said from his command post under the coffee table.

"Yeah, tell us about the time you crashed." Peter added the sound effects of an airplane whining to its doom, followed by an ear-shattering explosion.

"Grandpa crashed more than once, dummy," Mickey said.

"I'm telling Mom. You're not supposed to call people dummy."

"Hey, hey, hey! No stories until you guys quit your squabbling." They shot each other accusing looks but remained silent. "That's better. Now then, which crash did you mean, Pete?"

"The one by Lake Plathit."

"That's Lake *Placid*," Mike said, laughing, "and if you guys know all of my stories, why do I have to tell them again?"

"Pleeeease . . . ," Lori begged. "We like your stories, Grandpa. Just one more time?"

"OK, OK. Now, let's see . . . how does that story go again?"

"You had to fly to Lake Placid to pick up a charter."

"Oh, yeah. That's right. Well, when I started out that day the weather report at Adirondack airport didn't sound too good, calling for broken cloud cover at about 1,000 feet. But I decided I'd fly the Beech Bonanza up anyway and take a chance on being able to spot the airport through the clouds."

"You were flying VFR, right?" Mickey asked.

"That's right. I didn't fly on instruments back then. Anyway, I headed north and had pretty good flying conditions until I came to the Adirondacks just past Glens Falls. Then things got bad in a hurry. I should have turned back, I suppose, but I climbed above the clouds, instead, to get out of the bad weather. I figured I'd be able to spot Mount Marcy above the cloud cover, then I could watch for Whiteface Mountain just north of Marcy. The airport is about 15 miles or so due west of Whiteface.

"But about the time I figured I should be getting close to Mount Marcy, there was a solid bank of clouds below me and no mountains visible at all. I couldn't even spot Marcy, and it's more than 5,000 feet high! Well, I kept heading due north, hoping for a break in the clouds so I could at least find out where I was, but before long I began to realize that I was lost. There was just no way I could descend through that soup to look for Adirondack airport, not with all those 3,000- and 4,000-foot peaks hiding under the gray stuff! Plattsburg and Burlington airports had both reported worse weather conditions than Adirondack airport, so I finally decided the only thing I could do was turn around and head back to Warren County airport near Glens Falls before my fuel got any lower.

"I banked around to head south again when I thought I smelled oil smoke. I checked the instrument panel, which I'd been ignoring up 'til then, trying to see the ground, and that's when I knew I was in serious trouble. The oil pressure was nil and the temp gauges were both rising. By now the cockpit was filling with smoke, so I cut the engine and put the plane in a shallow glide. My altitude was only about 7,000 feet, and I knew Mount Marcy was down there somewhere, less than 2,000 feet below me."

"And you didn't have a parachute," Petey added.

"Nope, no parachute. I tried to keep the plane level and glide down as slowly as I could, all the time straining my eyes for a break in the clouds or for the dark shape of a mountain to come out at me."

"Were you scared, Grandpa?" Lori asked.

"You bet I was! My hands shook so badly I could hardly hold the stick. I tried to restart the engine a couple of times because sometimes you can make it in on just a couple of cylinders, but the engine was a goner. And I thought I was a goner too. The worst part was waiting—just falling and falling out of the sky, waiting for the end to come.

"Down I went, and at about 6,000 feet I entered the soup. It's an eerie feeling, you know, just gliding silently through the clouds with nothing visible outside the cockpit but gray fuzz. You have no sensation of falling when you're in the clouds and no sense of direction. The only way you know you're going down is by watching the altimeter unwind." He drew circles in the air with his forefinger.

"Five thousand feet. Four thousand feet. I was well

111

below minimum altitude by now, and I knew that any second I could slam into Mount Marcy or Porter or Allen Mountain, depending on where I was. All I could do was grit my teeth and brace for the impact of the crash that was sure to come.

"Three thousand feet. Two thousand feet. I could hardly believe I was still alive! Then all of a sudden—*whoosh!* I broke through the cloud cover and saw mountains on either side of me and the northern tip of Lake Placid dead ahead of me. I had been skimming along right down the valley between the peaks, just missing Whiteface on one side and Moose Mountain on the other. My heart nearly jumped out of my chest, but now I knew at least I had a fighting chance of coming out of it alive if I could just set her down someplace. I was wringing wet with sweat, but I joined the living again.

"Now, Lake Placid is a fairly big lake, maybe four or five miles long, so I decided to steer the Bonanza down along the eastern edge where there weren't too many rocks and trees and maybe land close to the shoreline. I didn't have pontoons, but I glided her in just as if I did and, boy, did it ever feel good to touch down again!"

"But the plane flipped over, right?" Mickey asked.

"Yeah, it nosed over on me after I landed, but I unhooked my seat belt and walked away without a scratch—very, very glad to be alive."

Lori hugged him tightly. "I'm glad you didn't die, Grandpa."

"Me too!" Mike said, laughing. "I kept thinking about your grandma as I was going down, and about your dad and Uncle Mike. What would they do if anything happened to me? Your dad was about Mickey's age, and Uncle Mike was about 12, I think."

"Why did Grandma and Uncle Mike have to die?" Lori asked. "I never even got to meet them."

"Well, dying's just a part of life, Princess. Everyone has to die sooner or later. I've had a couple of close calls, like the one over Lake Placid, but it wasn't my time to go yet." He gently brushed a wisp of hair off her forehead. "I guess your grandma and Uncle Mike ran out of time."

"But what happens after you die?"

Mike drew a deep breath. He wished he had an answer for her, one that would sustain her through her grief in the months ahead. But he didn't know the answers himself. He tried to remember what his wife had believed about death, how she had consoled him when they got word that Mike Jr. was dead in Vietnam. Where had her courage and strength come from during the last months of her illness? It was too long ago. He couldn't remember.

"Well, I really don't know what happens, Lori," he said at last. "Once someone dies they can't exactly come back to tell everyone about it. But your grandma was a real good woman. She always went to church every week, and she believed that you go to heaven when you die and live up in the clouds with God."

"I don't like God. He makes people die."

"That's no way to talk, honey. I think God must be a pretty good guy. I always figured He was the One who steered my plane between the peaks that day. But sooner or later everyone's time to die finally comes, and there's nothing we can do about it."

"Will we see each other again after we're all dead?"

"I won't lie to you, Princess. I honestly don't know."

A heavy sadness settled over Mike's heart and a nameless apprehension and dread. It was the same sense of foreboding he had felt in the Adirondacks as he descended blindly through the clouds, waiting for the impact, wondering where he was heading and what was going to happen to him. But he felt an even deeper sadness for his grandchildren. He had nothing to leave behind with them—no assurances, no comfort, no consolation for their grief.

He knew he would have to end his life soon. The effects of his disease had started to show. But as he studied the little faces he loved so dearly, he longed to leave them hope and reassurance. For their sakes, he wished he could find the answers to their questions before he died.

7

Monday October 5, 1987

Wilhelmina sat at her kitchen table surrounded by tall piles of her brother's books. A damp, musty smell emanated from some of the older ones that had once been her father's. She wrinkled her nose with distaste.

She had been sitting here, staring into space, for well over an hour, listening to her grandmother's antique clock as it ticked off the seconds in the quiet house. She hadn't opened Peter's books. They held no answers for Mike. Her Bible lay open before her as well, but she could find no starting place, no point of juncture between the teachings of Jesus and the life of Mike Dolan.

What would Jesus say to him? "Mr. Dolan, you're going to die soon. Do you want to spend eternity in hell?" Or maybe, "You'd better hurry up and get saved, brother, before it's too late." She'd heard similar phrases used within her evangelical circle, but they didn't sound like Jesus' words to Wilhelmina.

She felt so helpless and inexperienced. Would she even get the opportunity to speak with Mike again? It would be much too forward of her to knock on his door uninvited. Should she reschedule the piano tuning? Dream up a new excuse?

The telephone jarred her out of her thoughts. It was Carol.

"Hello, Wilhelmina. How are you, dear? Listen, I'm calling to tell you that I can't go to the ballet with you this weekend. My sister and her husband are driving up from Virginia to stay for a week. I hope you can find somebody to go with you. Maybe Ellen Stockman would like my ticket."

This was the answer to Wilhelmina's prayers. It was perfect. Mike had confessed that he'd never been to the ballet the same day she admitted that she'd never flown a kite. Well, now that she'd flown a kite, he *had* to go to the ballet. They were performing "Romeo and Juliet." What better introduction to the subject of death and suicide than Prokofiev's beautiful, tragic ballet? Yes, it was perfect.

After she hung up the phone, Wilhelmina dialed Mike's number at the airport before she had time to change her mind. She recognized Mike's cheerful voice.

"Well, hi there, Professor. Long time, no see. Don't tell me, let me guess . . . you've decided to take me up on my offer and go flying with me."

"Well, no. Not exactly." She was surprised to find that she was smiling.

"I'm sorry to hear that. What can I do for you, then?"

"You can come to the ballet with me this Sunday afternoon."

"The ballet!"

"Yes. You said you've never been to one, and I just happen to have two tickets, so if you're not busy Sunday . . ." She ran out of words suddenly, and there was an uncomfortable silence.

"I'm speechless!" Mike finally said.

"I've decided not to take 'no' for an answer, so you may as well stop dreaming up excuses and come with me."

Mike laughed his hearty, contagious laugh. "Where have I heard that line before? OK, Professor, I guess you got me there."

"Good. Then it's settled. Why don't you come to my house around one o'clock, and we can drive over to Hartford in my car?" Wilhelmina wanted to make it clear she had no desire to repeat her ride in Mike's pickup truck.

"Hartford! Say, we could cut the trip down to no time at all if we flew."

"No," she said quickly, "I think I'd rather drive."

"OK, this is your party. I'll be there Sunday at one."

By Sunday, Wilhelmina's nerves vibrated like opening night at Carnegie Hall. This was it, her big debut, the opportunity God had provided for her to talk to Mike Dolan about his eternal soul. She could not—she dared not—fail Him this time. She may not have another chance.

She had read through all four of the Gospels this week in preparation and had tried to memorize some of the key passages, writing them out on index cards, which she carried in her purse. She'd hardly paid attention to Pastor Stockman's sermon that morning—something about "let the little children come to me . . ." She had no time to worry about kids. Her mission was Mike. She reviewed the memory verses on her index cards instead. *John 3:16, "For God so loved the world . . ."*

By the time the service had drawn to a close, Wilhelmina had begun to tremble. During the stillness of the closing prayer she accidentally stepped on one of the organ pedals, creating a rumbling, thundering noise that jarred the congregation out of their seats. Many of them probably believed the Second Coming had arrived. She'd never done such a thing before in all her years as organist, but Wilhelmina had been in too great a hurry to be embarrassed. She drove straight home to change for the ballet.

She was upstairs in her big front bedroom at five minutes to one when she heard Mike's noisy pickup truck pull into her driveway. Wilhelmina took a deep breath and mumbled a quick prayer. The doorbell rang. She hurried downstairs to let him in.

But when she opened the front door Mike wasn't there. Instead, his little granddaughter stood on the step in a ruffled pink dress and shiny patent leather shoes.

"Hi, Professor Brewster," she said shyly.

Wilhelmina's mouth fell open, but she couldn't make a sound. She caught a quick glimpse of Mike's truck backing out of her driveway.

"What? . . . Where? . . ." Wilhelmina was too startled to be coherent. When she realized the awful truth, that Mike was gone, leaving his granddaughter behind, Wilhelmina's disappointment came out in a groan. "Oh no!"

The little girl's smile faded. Her bottom lip began to quiver.

"I'm sorry," Wilhelmina said quickly. "It's just that . . . I mean . . . oh, never mind! Come in."

The child didn't move. Wilhelmina knew she'd been rude, but she didn't know how to make things right. She had never fussed much with children, even her own nieces and nephews. But apparently she was stuck with this child for the afternoon, and it made her furious. She attempted a smile, but her voice was brusque.

"Come in, child! I've forgotten your name."

"Lori," she said in a whisper.

"That's right. Come in, Lori." She took the girl's arm and pulled her into the house. Lori's terror-stricken expression made Wilhelmina feel like the wicked witch inviting Hansel and Gretel into her house for gingerbread. She led the way into the living room and watched as Lori gazed at the huge front hall and spacious rooms with awe.

"Sit down." It sounded more like a command than an invitation. Lori obediently sat, perching tentatively on the edge of the sofa cushion as if ready to run. "Would you like a cookie or something?" Lori shook her head. This was going rather badly. Wilhelmina decided to start over.

"I'm sorry for treating you rudely, Lori. It's just that you took me by surprise. I was expecting your grandfather, you see."

"He had to give a flying lesson."

"A flying lesson! Couldn't that have waited one more day?" Wilhelmina spoke without thinking, venting her anger. She'd been a fool for thinking Mike would go to the ballet with her. When she thought of all the planning and preparation she had done for this day and how it was all going to go to waste, she wanted to weep.

"Grandpa tried to call, but you weren't home. He said you wouldn't mind if I came to see the ballet instead of him." Lori's eyes shone with tears. Wilhelmina knew she had to quench her anger, for Lori's sake.

"Of course, I don't mind. Have you ever been to the ballet before?"

Lori shook her head.

"Well, I think you'll like it."

They sat opposite each other in uncomfortable silence, listening to the clock on the mantel ticking loudly. It was a 40-minute drive to downtown Hartford. What on earth could they talk about all that way? She wished she'd paid closer attention to the sermon.

When the telephone rang, Wilhelmina hurried to the kitchen to answer it with relief. It turned out to be a salesman for a carpet cleaning service, but she listened to his entire sales pitch with great interest before finally getting rid of him. When she returned to the living room Lori stood in front of the grand piano, gently stroking the smooth ivory keys.

"Do you play?" Lori jumped at the sound of Wilhelmina's voice and quickly turned to face her, wearing the expression of a startled fawn staring into the headlights of an oncoming car. She didn't blame the child for being afraid of her.

"Well, go ahead. You may play it if you'd like." Lori shook her head. "Oh, here . . . like this." Wilhelmina sat down at the piano and played part of a simple etude, her fingers flowing expertly over the familiar keyboard.

"That's beautiful," Lori said when she finished. "I wish I could play like that."

"Well, no one ever learned to play the piano by wishing. Why don't you take lessons then?"

"Daddy says they're a waste of money."

"I see. Do you have a piano at home?"

"No, but Grandpa does at his house. He can't play it, though. It used to be my Grandma Dolan's."

Lori caressed the piano's smooth black wood as she talked. She was smearing the finish with fingerprints, but Wilhelmina bit her tongue. She had to keep the child interested in something or the afternoon would be unbearable.

"Sit down, Lori. I'll give you a quick piano lesson."

Lori sat down on the far edge of the bench. Wilhelmina wondered how she kept from falling off.

"Like this, Lori. Keep your posture erect, fingers arched, wrists up, elbows loose. Try it."

Lori shook her head, apparently overwhelmed by Wilhelmina's stern commands. She had worked with college students for so many years that she no longer remembered how to handle a beginner. Why, oh why, had Mr. Dolan done this to her? Why couldn't the afternoon have gone as she had planned it?

Wilhelmina exhaled. She'd better back up. How had she started piano lessons as a beginner, so many years ago? Her first piano teacher had been Mrs. Schumann, a sweet, smiling housewife with reddish-blond hair who had once sung in the opera in her native Germany. Her tiny, gingerbread-like cottage was always spotlessly clean and smelled of warm apples and cinnamon. One of her three towheaded daughters often stood beside the piano as Mrs. Schumann taught, silently listening to Wilhelmina practice her scales.

Mrs. Schumann had made music fun by giving little names and personalities to everything. Mrs. Treble Clef lived in one house, and Mr. Bass Clef lived across the street from her. Quarter notes were little bunny rabbits hopping along in quick little jumps, and whole notes were sleepy brown bears, ambling slowly down the scale.

"Don't break the egg, Wilhelmina," she would say with a chuckle to remind her to keep her fingers arched. She hadn't thought of Mrs. Schumann for a long, long time. Wilhelmina summoned all her reserves of patience and tried again.

"Let me see you sit up nice and straight and tall, Lori. Good. Now, only the tips of your fingers touch the keys, see? This part of your hand and your wrists stay up. Pretend there's an egg under your hand and you don't want to break it."

Lori giggled. Wilhelmina began to relax.

"That's right. Now, only your thumbs can lie on their sides. They're rather sleepy fellows, see?"

Lori mimicked whatever Wilhelmina showed her, catching on quickly. Before long, the teacher in Wilhelmina took over, and she lost her self-consciousness.

"As you can see, there are white keys and black keys. Today we'll start with the white ones. Each one has a name. This one is middle C. Now you play it."

Lori sounded the note with her index finger. Her ragged fingernails were painted with chipped pink nail polish.

"Good. Play it again."

As Lori sounded the note again, Wilhelmina opened one of her music books and propped it on the rack.

"Now all of these keys—these notes—can be found on the music score. Some of them live in this house on top, with Mrs. Treble Clef. She has a high, tinkly voice, like this." She played a short tune in the upper registers. "And some of the notes live down in this house with Mr. Bass Clef. He has a very deep voice, like this." She played a rumbling tune in the lower registers. Mr. Middle C rides his car here, between the two houses."

Lori was at ease now and enjoying the lesson. The awkwardness between them was nearly gone. Wilhelmina had begun to expound on how "every-good-boy-deserves-fudge" when she suddenly remembered the time.

"Goodness, child! The ballet!" She consulted her watch, then hurriedly gathered her purse and gloves.

"Did it start already?"

"No, we'll make it on time. But we'll have to hurry."

The drive to Hartford went better than Wilhelmina expected. Lori chatted happily about the third grade, her friends at school, and her two "dumb" brothers.

"You know, Lori, I also have two brothers. And I was born in the middle, too, like you were." She smiled to herself, remembering. Laurentius was tall and serious, towering over her with his dark, Puritanical scowl. He always had to be the organizer, the leader, the boss. And blond, good-natured Peter. Everyone loved Peter. Whenever he entered a room it was as if someone had finally turned on the lights.

"Mickey always thinks he's the boss," Lori said. "He tries to order me around all the time, just because he's older. I hate that. Did your older brother think he was a hot shot too?"

"Oh, yes! And you know what? He still does."

Laurentius had phoned several days ago to offer his authoritative advice on how Wilhelmina should spend her retirement. She knew Peter had talked to him after her visit to New Haven, and it infuriated her. How dare they discuss her life behind her back? It was none of their business!

"And Petey is such a baby sometimes," Lori said.

"He always has to have his own way. Mom spoils him like crazy."

"My younger brother is named Peter too," Wilhelmina said in surprise.

"Did your mom spoil him a lot?"

"It certainly seemed that way sometimes. Peter still loves to be the center of attention."

"Do your brothers play the piano too?"

"No. That was my own special territory, something that only I could do. Larry played the violin for a while and Peter the French horn, but they didn't stay with it once they were out of school. I could play circles around them, and they were both quite jealous of that." She smiled as she remembered the fierce competition between the three of them in all areas of their lives, especially for their father's approval. But she had excelled far beyond her brothers in music.

"I wish I could play like you. I'd sure show my stupid brothers!"

"Oh dear. That's hardly a proper motivation to take up the piano." But Lori's attitude seemed painfully familiar to her. Could this be part of the reason for her depression since retiring? Had she used her musical talent all these years to win her father's approval and feel as worthy as her distinguished brothers? If so, it would help explain why she felt so utterly lost without her profession. She glanced at Lori and felt strangely grateful to her.

They arrived at the concert hall in time for Wilhelmina to read the program notes to Lori above the clamor of the orchestra as it warmed up in the pit. When the house lights dimmed, a hush of anticipation fell over the audience. Then the curtain rose to reveal the glittering ballroom of the Capulet mansion. Through open French doors, a golden moon shone above a little pond. The water rippled in the evening breeze. Lori gasped in wonder and delight.

For months Wilhelmina had been unable to attend a concert without feeling resentful and depressed. But today she watched the dancers through Lori's eyes and heard the music through Lori's ears. They were both entranced. Lori didn't fidget or grow bored. She sat perfectly still, watching breathlessly, and when it ended she had tears in her eyes.

"That was the most beautiful thing I ever saw in my whole life!" she said as they got back into Wilhelmina's car. "I wanted it to go on forever and ever."

"I did too," Wilhelmina said, and it was the truth. She thought of her friend Carol, who often fell sound asleep during a matinee. Wilhelmina would have to nudge her awake if she started to snore. "I'm very glad you came with me today, Lori."

"Then you're not mad at Grandpa anymore?"

Mike. Wilhelmina hadn't thought about him all afternoon. But now that Lori reminded her, the queasy knot of apprehension returned to the pit of her stomach.

"I wasn't mad at him, Lori, it's just that . . ." How could she explain to this child the divine compulsion that urged her to share the gospel with Mike? Or the

126

feeling of near despair at her failure to do so? The ballet ticket had seemed heaven-sent, and she didn't know how she would ever arrange another opportunity to talk to him. Wilhelmina knew she was running out of time.

Mike finished the preflight checks on his Beechcraft Staggerwing as the brightly painted Rainbow Society van pulled up near the hangar. He wiped his hands on his coveralls and walked over to greet the driver, a petite, cheerful woman in her 40s.

"Hello, Mr. Dolan, I'm Ann Wilson. We talked on the phone this morning."

"Yes. Nice to meet you, Ma'am."

"I want to apologize again for giving you such short notice. I hope we didn't spoil any plans you had for today, but . . ." Her voice dropped to a whisper. "Ryan's leukemia is no longer in remission. The doctors expect a very rapid decline."

"No apologies necessary. I understand." She had no idea how well he understood. "My plane is ready whenever you are."

Mrs. Wilson slid open the van door and lowered a frail boy in a wheelchair down by hydraulic ramp. A nurse and another woman, probably the boy's mother, hovered nearby.

"Mr. Dolan, this is Ryan Mitchell and his mother, Cathy."

"Glad to meet you. Come right this way, the plane's all ready to fly."

A stout nurse in a crisp uniform wheeled Ryan across the tarmac to the Beechcraft. Mike lifted him into the left-hand seat of the cockpit. He felt as light as air, his bones ready to poke through his pale skin.

"Is this your first lesson, Ryan?"

"Yeah."

"Well, the pilot always sits here on the left. Are you ladies coming too?" Ryan's mother and the nurse stood beside the plane, waiting for Mike to help them on board.

"No!" Ryan shook his head emphatically. "I don't want them to. I want to go alone. Just me and Mr. Dolan."

Mike remembered the humiliation and helplessness he felt after his last cancer surgery. He'd hated having everyone hovering around him too. He draped his arm around Mrs. Mitchell's shoulder and gently steered her away from the plane.

"Let me take him up alone, all right? We'll be fine. If there's any problem, I promise we'll land right away."

He waved his cap and quickly climbed into the copilot's seat, shutting the door before anyone could argue. He gave Ryan a wink and a thumbs up. Ryan grinned as the ladies retreated to the van.

"OK, now. Before we take off I want you to get familiar with all the controls."

"I already know most of them. That's the turn and bank indicator and that's the altimeter."

"Hey, that's right!"

"I have a flight simulator on my computer, so I fly all the time."

"That's great. You're way ahead of the game then."

"I really wanted to fly a jet."

"So I heard! Actually, they're basically the same, but it's a lot easier to learn on a small aircraft. Most jet pilots start out just like this, you know. If you make a mistake at 150 miles an hour, you've got a little more time to correct it than you do at Mach 1."

"Yeah, I guess you're right. I crashed on my simulator all the time when I was first learning."

"Well, try to remember that this is for real, OK?" Mike said with a grin.

"No sweat, Mr. Dolan."

"OK. Let's run through the instruments quickly, then we'll grab some sky."

Mike gave Ryan a quick overview of the instrument panel and the controls. It was the fastest first lesson he'd ever given, and he probably broke several aviation regulations, but judging by what Mrs. Wilson said, Ryan would probably never get a second lesson, much less his pilot's license. The Rainbow Society granted dying children their last wishes.

"Ready to take off?"

Ryan's face was bright with excitement. "Yeah!"

He helped Ryan guide the plane away from the hangar and contact the control tower. They were assigned runway zero two, the one Mike usually used with beginners. He showed Ryan how to prepare for takeoff.

"All set?" he asked again. Ryan nodded. Mike saw the thrill of anticipation in Ryan's eyes, and he relived his own first lesson with Joe Donovan.

"Give it more throttle . . . that's it . . . keep her pointed straight ahead . . . watch your air speed indicator . . . now, ease the yoke back . . . good . . . good . . ."

Mike felt the glorious sensation of weightlessness as the little plane lifted off the runway.

"Great, Ryan! That simulator taught you well."

"The real thing is awesome!"

"You sound like my oldest grandson. He's about your age. We're going to climb to 4,000 feet, then I'll let you take the controls again, OK?"

"OK. Does your grandson fly too?"

"Yep. Mickey's a real good little pilot. Learns fast."

"Has he ever gone solo?"

"Not yet. We're taking that part kind of slow. It's more than just ability at the controls that counts. He's landed and flown lots of times with his dad or me sitting here watching him, but he's not mature enough to go solo yet. Airplanes are pretty expensive toys."

When they got to their cruising altitude, Mike let Ryan take the controls again. He had a great time, soaring through the clouds and learning how to gently bank and turn. But after half an hour he seemed bored.

"Can you teach me to do a loop or a barrel roll, Mr. Dolan?"

"Whoa! Don't you think that complicated stuff better wait? At least until the second lesson?"

"I'll probably never get another lesson," Ryan said quietly. "I'm going to die."

Mike's smile faded. "Yeah, so I heard. That's a real shame. I'll tell you something, though. I've given lots of lessons, and I can see you'd make a mighty fine pilot. You've got a natural feel for it, and that's the truth." He glanced at Ryan and sighed. "I'll let you in on a little secret, if you promise not to tell anyone."

"I promise."

"I'm dying too."

"For real?"

"Yep, for real. The doctor said I had three to six months. But that was almost a month ago, so—"

"How come?"

"Cancer. I had a tumor removed a few years back, but now it's spreading."

"That's rough."

"I figured you'd understand." They looked at each other and grinned, cementing the bond. They flew in comfortable silence for several minutes, savoring the magnificent view, the joyous freedom of flight, the contentment that comes with understanding.

"You scared about it, Mr. Dolan?"

"Yeah, sometimes. Are you?"

"Maybe a little. Mostly I'm just sick and tired of all the junk the doctors put me through, you know? I just want to be left in peace."

"I know. They mean well, Ryan. They're only trying to help."

"What do you think it'll be like . . . dying?"

131

"I think it'll be a lot like flying. Like that wonderful feeling of freedom you get when you finally break free from the earth and lift off. I guess we'll find out soon enough. What do you think it'll be like?"

"Probably no more pain. And I'll feel really good again."

They both fell silent. Mike gazed down at the magnificent rolling hills beneath them. For as often as he'd flown, he'd never grown tired of seeing the world from above. Each time thrilled him like the first. How he loved this beautiful earth and all the precious people in his life.

"Mr. Dolan?"

"Yeah, Ryan?"

"What difference does it make then? About the loops and barrel rolls, I mean?"

"I don't follow you."

"Suppose you were to teach me to do a loop. What's the worst thing that could happen?"

Mike considered a moment, then laughed out loud. "I see what you mean. There's not much for either of us to worry about, is there?" He made up his mind. "OK. We'll start with a loop."

"All right!"

"See if you can find a road or something we can line up with down below, for reference."

"Like that highway over there?"

"That's perfect. Can you bank around and line up with it?" He coached Ryan through each step until they were aligned with the highway.

132

"Now, a loop isn't hard to do, but it *is* hard to do right. I'll do the first one so you can get the feel of it. First I start a shallow dive . . . Then, I pick up a little speed . . . Now, always check the altimeter reading as you start to pull up. Push the throttle gradually forward . . . Feel the G forces?"

"Yeah! Cool!"

"Keep the ailerons and rudder centered. The air speed is dropping now, but you want to have just enough speed to keep us in our seats."

"We're upside down!"

"Yep. See the horizon up there behind us?"

"Oh, wow! My mom would freak out!"

"Good thing she didn't come. Now, you don't want to rush the loop. Your nose should coast downward as the speed begins to pick up again. Keep the wings level . . . and . . ."

"We did it!"

"Quick, check the altimeter. If we've done it right, we should level out at the same altitude we started."

"It's the same!" The plane bumped suddenly, like a car hitting a pothole. "Whoa . . . what was that?"

"We just passed through our own wake."

"That's awesome! Are you really going to let me try one now, Mr. Dolan?"

"Can you stay cool and not panic?"

"I think so."

"Let's go for it! What have we got to lose?"

Wilhelmina was grateful for the long stretch of four-lane highway as she switched the car to cruise control. Her mind wasn't on her driving or the magnificent fall foliage all around them. Tomorrow was Monday. A new week. An endless week, with nothing to look forward to. The heavy weight of depression slipped over her shoulders again. Lori's voice interrupted her thoughts.

"I didn't like the way the ballet ended. Why did they both have to die?"

"There can't always be a happy ending. Life isn't like that. Dying is a natural part of life." She should be having this conversation with Mike.

"What happens when you die, Professor Brewster?"

"You go to heaven . . . paradise."

"And live in the clouds with the angels?"

"Yes, something like that. Lori, does your family belong to a church?"

"No. I used to go to Sunday School sometimes with my friend Melissa, but Daddy got mad and stomped around a lot whenever Mommy let me go, so I don't go no more."

"*Any* more." Wilhelmina corrected her automatically. "But, why? Do you know why your father got mad when you went to Sunday School?" She felt guilty for pumping Lori about her homelife, but if she wanted to help Mike, she needed to learn more about him.

"Daddy says Grandma Dolan used to make him and Uncle Mike go to church with her all the time, and he hated it. He says they teach a bunch of lies at Sunday School."

134

"Was your Uncle Mike the one who died in Vietnam?"

"Yeah, a long time ago. I only seen pictures of him."

"You *saw* pictures. What about your grandfather? Does he ever go to church?"

"No, but he got real mad at Daddy for saying they teach lies. He told Daddy not to say things like that. Then they both got mad and started shouting. Mickey said it was all my fault for making them get in a fight. That's why I don't want to go with Melissa no more."

"*Any* more. How long ago did this happen, Lori?"

"It was before Grandpa got cancer and went into the hospital for his operation. But I went with Melissa last Christmas to see the play about the Baby in the manger because she was an angel, and she wanted me to see her. She's my best friend. Mom said don't tell Daddy."

Wilhelmina slowly digested this new information about Mike and his family, wondering what to make of it all. She had considered inviting Lori to church but not if it meant family friction.

"Professor Brewster?" Lori's voice trembled slightly.

"Yes, dear?"

"Can you only go to heaven if you belong to a church?"

Wilhelmina gripped the steering wheel tighter. How could she possibly answer such a question in a way that an eight-year-old could understand? She wasn't trained for this sort of thing. Perhaps she should ask the Christian education director at her church to talk to

135

Lori. He'd know what to say. But the director wasn't here now, and Lori was waiting for an answer.

"Did someone tell you that, Lori? That you only go to heaven if you belong to a church?"

"When Grandpa got cancer and had to be operated on, Melissa said he better not die because he never went to church and . . ." Lori's voice broke and she sobbed out the rest through her tears. ". . . Melissa said Grandpa wouldn't go to heaven . . . that he'd go to hell . . . and burn forever in a lake of fire!"

The highway blurred in front of Wilhelmina. How could Christians be so cruel and thoughtless? How could they say such things? Then she remembered the tract that she had almost given to Mike. The one with the picture of hell-fire and brimstone. She silently thanked God for stopping her.

"Lori . . . listen to me, dear. Everyone in the world deserves to go to hell because no one is perfectly good. Even the people who go to church every week. If God judged everyone fairly, we'd all belong in hell . . . your grandpa, me, even Melissa. But God doesn't want anyone to go to hell. God loves you and me, and he loves your grandfather too. He wants all of us to be with Him in heaven, not in hell."

"Then why did God make hell?"

Another theological monstrosity to explain. Father devoted entire seminary lectures to this subject. How could Wilhelmina hope to explain it? She had to try.

"Do your mother and father punish you when you do something wrong, Lori? Let's say, you broke a

136

window or something. Wouldn't you have to pay for it?"

Lori nodded and swiped at her tears with the back of her hand. "Mickey broke the remote control for the TV when he was horsing around, and now Daddy says he's gotta pay for it out of his allowance."

"Well, God is like a father to us, and we have to pay for all the wrong things we've done. That's what hell is for. But do you remember the Baby in the manger at Melissa's Christmas play?"

"It was really just a doll, but it was supposed to be Baby Jesus."

"That's right. Well, Jesus is God's Son and He lived in heaven—"

"With the angels?"

"Yes, with the angels. Then He came down to earth as a baby and grew into a man, just to pay for all the bad things we've done. It would be like . . . like Jesus paying for a new remote control so that Mickey wouldn't have to. Because of Jesus, you and I and Melissa and your grandfather don't have to go to hell because Jesus took our punishment for us."

"But don't you have to go to church for Jesus to do that?"

Wilhelmina hesitated, a lifetime of strict doctrinal beliefs clinging to her like barnacles on a rusty old ship. "No, Lori. You don't have to go to church. You only have to believe in Jesus and tell Him you're sorry. Then ask Him to forgive you and to come into your heart. But we *should* go to church to worship

Him. To say 'thank You' for all that He's done for us. And to learn more about Him."

Wilhelmina rounded the last corner and pulled into her driveway. Mike's pickup was parked at the end of it. He was leaning casually against the tail gate.

"Grandpa's here!" Lori scrambled out of the car and flung herself into his arms. "Oh, Grandpa, it was so beautiful! You should've seen it!"

Yes, he should have. Wilhelmina's irritation at Mike returned, full strength.

"Maybe next time, Princess. That is, if the professor ever invites us again. Did you remember to say thank you?"

"Thank you, Professor Brewster," she said dutifully, then she sprang to life once more. "Grandpa, you know what? She gave me a piano lesson. I want to learn to play just like she does. Can I, Grandpa? Can I take piano lessons? Please?"

"You don't even own a piano."

"But you do, and I could practice at your house. Please, Grandpa?"

"You have to ask your mom and dad, Princess. It's up to them, not me."

"But I don't want to ask Daddy. He'll say no. Please, Grandpa? Can't you ask him?"

Mike looked at Wilhelmina helplessly. The words tumbled out of her mouth before she could stop them. "I would be happy to teach her, Mike, if her parents don't mind. We can work out a price they can afford."

Was she going totally crazy? Taking on a beginning

student, with no musical background? Her brother Larry would say it was beneath her. A waste of her talent. But it was the only way she could think of to see Mike again.

"I'll ask him, Princess. That's all I can promise. Hop in the truck now, and I'll be there in a minute, all right?"

"Bye, Professor Brewster. I'll remember the part about holding the egg."

Mike took Wilhelmina's arm and led her around behind the truck. He would probably try to apologize and make excuses. She stiffened with anger.

"I want to thank you for taking her with you today, Willymina. We're just simple folks, you know, and we don't go to many cultural things like that. I figured she'd really enjoy it."

"Yes. She did."

Mike twirled his Yankee's cap for a moment before looking up at her. He wasn't what anyone would call handsome, probably never had been, but there was a warmth in his smile and a gentleness in his clear blue eyes that somehow made him attractive.

"I get the feeling you're kind of mad at me for not going today, Professor."

"Lori said you were giving a flying lesson. Couldn't it have waited one more day?"

"Well . . . no, Ma'am. It couldn't." He spoke quietly, "I didn't want Lori to know, you see, but the lesson was for a kid not much older than she is. He's dying of leukemia and this was his last wish, to fly an airplane. Well, he really wanted to fly a fighter jet, but I don't own any jets, so—"

"Oh, Mike, I'm so sorry. I—"

"No, no. I should have explained it to you, but there just wasn't much time, you see. The Rainbow Society called me this morning because Ryan was starting to go downhill and they had to arrange to get him out of the hospital and—"

"Please, Mike. Don't say any more. I feel terrible. The truth is, Lori and I had a wonderful time. Next time I'll get three tickets, and you can come too."

"I'd like that. Thanks again, Professor." He gave her arm a gentle squeeze and hopped into his truck. Lori waved out the window as they roared away.

Wilhelmina walked toward the house feeling totally drained. Piano lessons and flying lessons. Older brothers and younger brothers. Heaven and hell. It was only six o'clock, but she was going to take a hot bath and go straight to bed.

What was it about Mike Dolan? Every time Wilhelmina was with him he made her take a good look at herself. And Wilhelmina hated what she saw.

As she unlocked the back door she heard the kitchen phone ringing. She recognized her older brother's voice.

"I'm glad I finally caught you, Wilhelmina. Listen, it's about Homecoming weekend at the college next Saturday . . ."

Resentment flared in Wilhelmina at the mention of Faith College. The thought of being polite and sociable to the dean and all her former colleagues for an entire weekend filled her with dread. She did not want to go to Homecoming this year. But it would be the first year she had ever missed.

"Marge and I plan to drive down for the weekend," her brother's deep bass voice droned on.

"Of course, Larry. And you can spend the night here if you'd like." There was a long pause on the other end.

"Are you sure?"

"Yes, I'm sure. You stay with me every year, don't you? Why would you even need to ask such a question?"

"Well, because you sound a little . . . upset."

"It's been a long afternoon. I just got back from the ballet in Hartford. I'm tired, that's all. Tell Marjorie I'll have the guest room ready and I'll see you both on Saturday for lunch."

But Wilhelmina had just decided she would not set foot on that campus Homecoming weekend.

8

Saturday, October 17, 1987

When Wilhelmina awoke the following Saturday she felt like she'd spent the night inside her piano with all 88 hammers pounding against her head. She wished it meant she was getting the flu—anything to give her an excuse to stay home from the festivities at the college.

Larry would never understand why she didn't want to go. He would badger her about her duty and her responsibilities, pressuring her with guilt until she would finally paste on a phony smile and agree to go with him. Wilhelmina had never won an argument with him in her life. When Homecoming ended and Larry went back to his fancy church in Springfield, she'd be depressed for weeks.

She took two pills for her headache and found clean sheets for the bed in the guest room. If only she had a legitimate excuse to stay home, one that Larry couldn't possibly argue with. She was still searching for one when the telephone rang.

"Hi, there, Professor. Mike Dolan here. I hope I'm not disturbing you or anything." It felt good to hear Mike's voice, in spite of her lingering guilt for failing to witness to him.

"Why, no. You're not bothering me at all! What can I do for you, Mike?"

"Well, I hope you were serious about giving Lori those piano lessons, because she hasn't given her father or me a moment's peace since last Sunday."

"Of course I was serious. Did her father agree?"

"After a little arm-twisting. What I wanted to ask you, see . . . well, I offered to give Helen's old piano to Lori, but I'm not really sure if it's still any good."

"Would you like me to take a look at it?"

"I would really appreciate it, if you don't mind. No one has played on it in years."

"How about this afternoon?"

"Well, I don't want to bother you if you have other plans. There's no big hurry."

"Actually, this afternoon would work out very well for me."

"Great! OK, then, how about if I pick you up around one?"

"I can drive over, Mike. I don't mind."

"No, I don't want you wasting any gas on my account. I'll pick you up around one." He hung up before she could argue.

Wilhelmina hummed to herself as she finished making the guest bed. Another ride in Mike's truck wasn't half as bad as trying to be sociable at Faith College all afternoon. She had a valid excuse to stay home. That was all that mattered.

Laurentius and his wife, Marjorie, arrived with style and pomp later that morning. He swept grandly into Wilhelmina's house like visiting royalty and immediately took over. He reminded Wilhelmina more than ever of a great bald eagle, with his patrician nose and scowling, hooded eyes. Larry's towering presence overshadowed his plump, gray-haired wife. Marjorie took the biblical injunction for wives to be submissive to their husbands quite literally, and as far as Wilhelmina knew, had never ventured an original opinion in her life. Nor was she ever likely to as long as she was married to Larry, the world's foremost authority on any issue.

The Reverend Dr. Laurentius Horatio Brewster, B.D., M.Div., Th.D., had successfully shepherded wayward sinners into the heavenly kingdom for more than 45 years. During lunch, Wilhelmina decided to mine his vast resources of knowledge for a few pointers on how to witness to Mike. But she would have to be careful to keep the questions general or Larry would begin asking questions of his own. She passed the platter of ham sandwiches.

"Larry, how much of your job involves ministering to those who are already Christians and how much involves reaching the unsaved?"

"Well, I have a rather large church to administer, as you know, so I've had to delegate many duties to my associates in specialized areas. In fact, I currently have a very competent minister of evangelism whose job it is to reach the unsaved."

"How does he do that? Does he go out on the highways and byways and round them up?"

"Of course not. It's a specialized field of theology now. They have a major in evangelism at the seminary."

Wilhelmina took this piece of news very hard. If ministers earned advance degrees in order to witness to unbelievers like Mike, how could she hope to do a good job of it? Her purse full of 3" x 5" cards suddenly seemed ridiculous compared to a seminary degree in evangelism.

"Let's suppose your minister of evangelism encountered an unbeliever . . . it doesn't matter how. What might he say to him? How would he begin?"

Larry took a bite of his sandwich and blotted his lips.

"Well, the first step would be to point out to this sinner his utter depravity, the debauchery and degradation of his immortal soul, the corruption and impurity—"

"Oh, good grief, Larry. We're not talking about an ax murderer. He's just an average man on the street."

He gazed at her patiently through half-closed eyes. "The Bible says in Rom. 3:23 that 'all have sinned and fall short of the glory of God.' So even your average man on the street is a vile, debased creature in God's eyes, worthy of the fiery punishments of hell and death—"

"Don't be so pompous! Mike isn't 'vile' or 'debased.'"

Larry smiled astutely. "Are we talking about a real person now?"

Wilhelmina wanted to swallow her own tongue. Larry had outsmarted her again. He wouldn't be satisfied now until he knew the whole story. She never should have brought up the subject in the first place. She passed him the platter of pickles, hoping to create a diversion, but Larry had stopped eating. His forkful of salad was poised in midair. He would continue to stare at her until she answered his question.

"Oh, all right! What if he is a real person? I still don't see why you have to start off by telling him he's vile and debased. He'd turn on his heel and walk away. And I wouldn't blame him one bit."

"Nevertheless, the truth must be spoken, Wilhelmina. Until he is shown the vast, yawning gulf that separates him from God and the fiery torments of

145

judgment that await him, this sinner will see no need for repentance or for a Savior."

Wilhelmina couldn't do it. She could never talk about moral depravity or hellfire and brimstone to Mike Dolan. She was sorry she had asked Larry for advice.

"Would anyone like some cake?" she asked, as Larry paused in his sermon.

Marjorie cleared her throat, a sign that she was, at last, about to speak. "I don't mean to rush you, Wilhelmina dear, but it's nearly one o'clock. Why don't you go get changed and I'll clean up the lunch dishes?"

Wilhelmina drew a deep breath. "I'm not going with you, Marjorie. I have another appointment."

Larry set down his fork. "Not going? Wilhelmina!"

"Listen, spare me your sermon on duty and responsibility, Larry. I'm not going and that's final. Faith Bible College will just have to celebrate without me. In fact, my ride will be here any minute, so you'll have to excuse me. Just leave the dishes, Marjorie. I'll do them later."

She gathered up the serving platters and started toward the kitchen door, but Larry rose from his place at the head of the table and stood in her path.

"What is all this nonsense?" He looked and sounded so much like Father that Wilhelmina wanted to laugh.

"Larry, who won the Homecoming game last year? Or the year before? Do you remember? Do you really care? It's a waste of time to go to those things, and I don't have time for it this year. I have another engagement."

Larry's stern demeanor transformed to one of pastoral compassion. He draped his arm around her shoulder. "I think I know what this little fuss is all about, Wilhelmina. Your pride has been wounded, hasn't it? And so you've decided to avoid Faith College this year. Now, we all have to face up to difficult situations from time to time, but the best way to deal with them is to take the bull by the horns, so to speak. Just pick yourself up, dust off your wounded pride, and—"

"This has nothing to do with wounded pride and bull's horns, Larry. I promised to test a piano for one of my students, and I think that's a little more important than a boring reception and a football game."

Larry sputtered wordlessly for a moment as he tried to cope with the outrage of having his sermon cut off. "Well! This must be an extraordinarily talented student to merit the sacrifice of your duties on Homecoming weekend!"

Wilhelmina recalled Lori's stubby fingers and chipped pink nail polish. "Oh, yes. She has great potential."

"But it shouldn't take you all day to look at a piano. You'll still be able to attend the alumni banquet with us later tonight, won't you." It wasn't a question, it was a command.

"Sure, Larry." She'd won her freedom for the afternoon and that meant a partial victory. As she turned to carry the dishes into the kitchen, she heard the noisy exhaust of Mike's pickup truck. He tooted the horn.

"That's my ride. I'll see you later." She dodged around her brother and set the dishes in the sink, hoping to make a swift departure. But Larry had glanced out the dining room window at Mike's truck, and he charged after Wilhelmina like an angry bull.

"Good heavens! It's . . . it's a *truck!*"

"Of course it's a truck, Larry. How else would you move a piano?"

"But you can't possibly ride in *that!* It's nothing but a rusted-out hulk! And it has *dogs* in it!"

As Wilhelmina opened the door she heard Buster and Heinz barking their loud greeting. For a moment she was tempted to tell Larry what a pompous snob he was. But then her conscience reminded her that her original opinion of Mike and his truck was not very different from her brother's.

"Yes, Larry, the truck has dogs in it. And you know what? They're not purebred either."

"I'm not tearing you away from your company, am I?" Mike gestured to the Lincoln Town Car, parked in Wilhelmina's driveway.

"On the contrary. You're rescuing me." Her cheeks were bright pink, and she seemed flustered. Mike hoisted her into the passenger seat beside his grandson, Mickey, then climbed into the driver's seat. He kept the truck idling in neutral.

"I don't mean to be nosy, but I can see by the license

plate that whoever it is drove down from Massachusetts."

"It's only my brother and his wife, and they're not here to visit me, anyway. They came down for Homecoming weekend at the college."

"Oh." That's why she'd been so eager to go with him today. As Mike shoved the gearshift into reverse and backed out of the driveway, he felt a wave of anger at the college officials and the heartless way in which they had rejected her. He didn't blame her for wanting to avoid that place. He whistled tunelessly as he drove across town, trying to decide what he could do to cheer her up.

"Are you really going to give my stupid sister piano lessons?" Mickey asked Wilhelmina.

"Whoa! That's no way to talk about your sister," Mike said.

"Aw, Grandpa. Lori's such an airhead. A real space cadet. She'll never learn to play the piano."

"You wouldn't be just a little bit jealous, now, would you?" he asked.

"No way." But Mike could tell by the way Mickey scrunched lower in the seat that he had struck a raw nerve.

"Just asking. Some kids might get their noses out of joint if their sister was getting something new—like a piano and piano lessons, for instance." Mickey folded his arms across his chest. "Professor Brewster told me that she has two brothers. I wonder if they ever got jealous of her for playing the piano?"

He looked over at Wilhelmina, hoping to draw her into the conversation, but when he saw the look of sadness that crossed her face he wished he could retract the question.

"I suspect they felt a bit jealous, at times," she said, studying her lap. "But they each have special skills that I don't have, so it evens out in the end." She looked up at Mickey. "I think you'd be happier if you allowed Lori to be herself and you concentrated on those talents that only you possess."

A few minutes later, Mike pulled up in front of his tiny bungalow. He led the way through the front door, proud that he had cleaned up. His house looked a lot neater than the last time Wilhelmina had visited. But in spite of the fact that there were no dirty socks or half-eaten sandwiches, it irritated him to discover that the dust on the piano bench was thick enough to carve his name in.

"I guess the maid forgot to dust." He pulled out his handkerchief and wiped it away. "Go ahead, Willymina. It's all yours."

"It's a lovely old upright and a good brand name. It should play just fine." She sat down and opened the lid to the keyboard, then plunged in with a dazzling display of skill, her hands covering the keyboard from one end to the other.

"Wow! I don't think it's been played like that in its entire life," Mike said when she finished. "It's probably wondering what hit it just now."

"It's a really fine instrument. It would be worth a

fair amount if you ever decide to sell it." She played part of another song that Mike vaguely recognized.

"It sounds more in tune than the one at the Cancer Center," he said with a grin.

Wilhelmina looked up at him. She was almost smiling. "Yes. So it does. But I'd still have it tuned, if I were you, after it's been moved to your son's house. I can give you Mr. Amato's phone number. He's very good, and his prices are reasonable."

She doodled around on the keyboard for another minute or two, as if reluctant to finish her job so soon, then experimented with the pedals for a while. Finally she lowered the keyboard lid and stood up. She picked up Helen's picture on top of the piano.

"Is this your wife? Lori told me she used to play the piano."

"She did but nothing like you. She mostly played by ear. Popular songs, Christmas carols, stuff like that. Whenever we'd have a gang over we'd get her to play, and we'd all sing along. Nothing fancy."

Mickey sighed with the impatience of youth. "Is she done, Grandpa? Can we go fishing now?"

"Yes, Mickey, I'm done. Your grandfather can take me home." She returned Helen's picture to its place.

Mike glared at his grandson. Wilhelmina would never agree to stay longer now that she knew Mike had other plans. He needed to cheer her up, but he didn't know what to do.

"Uh . . . what about music, Willymina? Shouldn't we buy Lori a book or something?"

"Not right away. And anyhow, I have plenty of books I can lend her." She picked up her purse and inched toward the door.

Mike couldn't take her home, knowing she would sit around all alone and depressed. But Wilhelmina would never agree to go fishing with them either.

"I, uh . . . I think there's some old sheet music inside the bench there. Would you mind having a look at it before you go? I'll be right back."

He ducked into the kitchen, grabbed a plastic grocery bag, and began stuffing whatever he could find into it. A package of frozen hot dogs. Half a loaf of bread. Four nearly-stale donuts. Three cans of soda pop. A squeeze bottle of mustard. An unopened bag of potato chips. Mike glanced at the roll of masking tape laying on the counter and considered bringing it along to stick over Mickey's mouth.

"Grandpa promised to take me fishing later," he heard Mickey telling her. He couldn't hear Wilhelmina's mumbled reply. "Yeah, that's why I'm glad it didn't take very long for you to check out the piano."

Mike tied the handles of the plastic bag together and strode into the living room with it.

"Is any of that old music any good?" he asked.

"Well, I wouldn't throw it out. You never know."

"That means it's junk, Mickey. OK, then. Let's take off."

He tossed the bag of food behind the front seat of the truck, loaded the dogs and everyone else on board, and drove off. Ten minutes later he zoomed past her turnoff.

"Wait a minute. You just drove past my street."

"Sorry, Ma'am, we're taking you captive. Scream all you want, but it won't do any good."

"But I really should be—"

"The captain and crew of this pirate ship are deaf to all pleas for mercy, aren't we, Mickey, my mate?"

Mickey scowled. "Huh?"

"See? What did I tell you." Mike glanced at Wilhelmina and saw her smiling slightly.

"Well, I guess as long as we're not gone too long . . ."

"Let me ask you something, Willymina, and I want a straight answer. Do you really want me to take you back home so you can go with your brother to all that hoopla over at the college?"

She was silent for a moment. "No. Not really."

"That's what I figured." He gave her a broad smile and sang a rusty chorus of "Yo Ho Ho and a Bottle of Rum."

"Mike . . . ," she said when he'd finished, "I . . . I just want to say thanks. For rescuing a damsel in distress."

They drove for almost an hour over narrow back roads, following the winding course of the river, until they came to a state park. A week or two ago it had probably looked spectacular, but now the fall leaves had passed their prime. The trees looked nearly bare, and the forest stood braced for the winter ahead. Mike pulled the truck into an empty parking lot.

"Looks like we're about the only ones here," he said. "I hope you've got your walking shoes on."

Wilhelmina had nylons on and rather expensive leather pumps with low heels. But like a prisoner making a frantic dash toward freedom, she didn't care whether she ruined her shoes or not. Mickey grabbed his fishing pole and jogged ahead with the dogs. Mike took her arm to steady her as she picked her way carefully down the narrow, rutted hiking trail.

"I'm sorry I'm so poky."

"Oh, that's all right. I don't suppose you get to do much hiking in the woods."

"Goodness, no! I can't even remember the last time."

They walked for a quarter of an hour, and all the time Wilhelmina kept her eyes glued to the path, careful to watch for tree roots, snakes, and other unnamed dangers. She was beginning to regret coming on this adventure. Suddenly Mike gave a great sigh of satisfaction.

"Ahhh . . . there's something about the contentment of the forest that has power to restore a person. Know what I mean?"

Wilhelmina scowled. "No. How can a forest be content?"

"Well, maybe if you'd quit worrying about seeing a snake or tripping up and took the time to look around, you'd see what I mean."

"It's rather hard to enjoy the walk, Mr. Dolan, when

the trail is so rough, and I don't have proper shoes."

"If you'll pardon my forwardness, Ma'am, I don't think it's the trail or the shoes that's bothering you. Now, I don't blame you for not wanting to go to the college today. But at the same time, it must be hard on you, thinking about all that you're missing out on. I think part of you wants to be there and part of you doesn't."

Mike barely knew her, yet he understood her better than her own brother did. Better than she understood herself. She blinked back tears and looked up for the first time at the canopy of trees above her. The bare branches seemed woven together in an intricate pattern like black lace. The deep blue sky stood out in contrast above them.

"How can you tell that the trees are content, Mike?" she asked quietly.

"Listen for a minute."

He pulled her to a stop, and she stood in silent amazement, listening to the deep, penetrating stillness all around them. The swaying silence of the trees played a counterpoint to the distant song of birds, the quiet gurgling of water, the rustling of dry leaves in the wind.

"Can't you almost hear them sigh with contentment, Willymina? And you never see trees arguing among themselves or trying to push each other around. They're satisfied just to live and grow and quietly change with the seasons."

They started walking again, and the stillness of the

forest and the music of the whispering leaves beneath her feet seemed like the rising crescendo of a magnificent symphony. By the time they reached a little picnic spot along the banks of the river, Wilhelmina's soul felt refreshed and at peace.

She sat at the picnic table while Mike and Mickey climbed down the embankment to the river's edge. She watched them bait the line and cast out into the middle of the river and listened to their murmuring voices as they talked about what kind of fish they would catch and the best bait to use. Once Mickey settled in with his gear, Mike climbed the bank again and sat beside her on the bench.

"Is it legal to fish in a state park?" she asked.

"He never catches anything," Mike whispered.

"Never? Then I'm surprised he still likes to go fishing."

"Well, he thinks he caught a couple of fish, you see."

"Why on earth would he think that?"

"Because I tied one or two that I caught onto his line when he wasn't looking. But never in a state park," he quickly added.

Wilhelmina thought of Dean Bradford's empty promises. "Do you think it's right to deceive Mickey like that and get his hopes up?"

Mike's smile faded. "Well, I never thought about it like that. I never meant to tell a lie or anything. I just wanted to encourage him to keep trying. I figured sooner or later he would catch something on his own if he kept at it."

"I'm sorry, Mike. I had no right to say that. You're a wonderful grandfather. Lord knows, I would have made an abysmal grandmother. I have no patience with children at all."

"Now, you wouldn't say that if you could see how Lori's been prancing around the living room on her tippytoes all week. She thinks you're the greatest."

They sat side by side, listening to the silence, watching Mickey patiently cast out his line, then reel it slowly in, over and over again. But the peaceful setting and calm stillness of the afternoon were lost on Wilhelmina as her mind churned with images of Faith College, and her heart mourned her loss.

Mike drew in a deep breath, then let it out slowly. "Ahhh . . . isn't that a lovely smell, Willymina? The forest . . . the moss and dry leaves . . . the earth? It's the richest perfume ever made."

Wilhelmina took a tentative sniff. "Yes, I guess it is rather nice. I hadn't noticed."

The wind picked up as the fall afternoon began to fade, and she shivered in her thin sweater. "Hey, you're cold," Mike said. "Here, take my jacket."

Before she could protest, he shrugged off his scruffy leather bomber jacket and draped it across her shoulders.

"Now you'll be cold."

"I'll build a fire." He scurried around the clearing, gathering fallen branches, breaking them into smaller pieces over his knee, piling them on a bare patch of ground beside the picnic table.

"Is it legal to build a fire in a state park?" she asked. "I don't know."

"Well, don't you think you should ask permission before you build one?"

Mike bit his lip, and she knew he was suppressing laughter. He strode over to the nearest tree and tapped respectfully on the trunk.

"Excuse me, sir. Do you mind if we build a fire here? My friend's feeling a bit chilly." He turned back to Wilhelmina, grinning broadly. "He said it was all right with him as long as we're careful."

Mike's little routine was so comical, his smile so infectious, her own question so ridiculous, that Wilhelmina couldn't help laughing out loud.

"You must think I'm a pompous bore."

"No, but I'm sure you think I'm a terrible scoundrel. Let's see, how many crimes have I committed today? Kidnapping, fishing illegally, leading a minor into a life of crime, building a fire in a prohibited area . . ."

Wilhelmina smiled. "Oh, be quiet and light your fire. You didn't kidnap me, I came willingly. And you can't be accused of fishing unless you actually catch something. Besides, I heard that tall gentleman over there give you permission to light your fire, so go ahead."

Mike quickly dug through all his pockets. "I can't! I don't have any matches!"

They both laughed so helplessly that Mickey left his fishing pole and scrambled up the bank. "What's so funny, Grandpa?"

"Mickey, stay up here with the professor for a

minute while I jog back to the truck to look for some matches."

Buster and Heinz took off ahead of Mike as if they'd understood exactly what he said. Mickey sank down on the picnic bench beside her and stared at the ground.

"You can go ahead and fish if you want to," Wilhelmina told him. "You don't have to stay up here with me."

"No, I'll stay. Grandpa wants me to." Mickey appeared glum, as if resigned to a terrible fate. He sat with his elbows on his knees, his head propped in his hands.

"Well, that's a very responsible attitude for a young man to have."

"I'm the oldest. Everyone expects you to be responsible when you're the oldest. It's OK for Pete to fool around and do dumb things because he's the baby, but when I do something—even when it's an accident, like breaking the TV remote control thing—my dad says, 'You'll have to pay for that. We expect you to act your age!' Pete and Lori get away with way more than I do. I always have to watch out for Peter and take care of Lori . . . and she's such an airhead. Sometimes I wish I wasn't the oldest."

He scooped up a fistful of gravel and began pitching stones toward the river. Wilhelmina couldn't help thinking of her older brother. Father made Larry responsible for walking her and Peter to school and back. He was expected to have a paper route and to deliver his early morning papers in all sorts of weather. He was told to be the man of the house during Father's long preaching tours. Larry had been born a little adult, and Wilhelmina couldn't remember him ever being a carefree, skipping child. No wonder he still felt he had to take charge of every situation. She studied Mickey's solemn face as he pitched his last stone into the river.

"You know, Mickey, I've never gone fishing in my life. I don't know the first thing about it. But if you wouldn't mind helping me climb down the riverbank in these dreadful shoes, I think I'd like to learn."

"Sure! Come on, Professor." He took her hand and led her toward the path to the river. "Maybe you should take your shoes off and slide down the bank. It's nice and sandy."

She hesitated, then kicked them off. Mickey took both her hands and towed her to the bottom of the riverbank. Wilhelmina felt a peculiar sensation, like hundreds of insects scrambling up her legs, as her toes ripped through her nylons and the runs raced to the top of her pantyhose. But at least she'd reached the bottom of the hill without breaking any bones.

"Now what do I do?"

"First you have to put the bait on the hook." Mickey whipped the fishing pole around and snagged the front of Wilhelmina's sweater with the hook, tearing a large hole.

"Oh, *no!* I'm sorry!" His panicky attempts to free her caused more of the sweater to unravel. His face was a portrait of despair.

"It's all right, Mickey. I always hated this sweater anyway. Here, let me get it." She managed to twist the hook free, but the jagged hole in her sweater was irreparable. It would go into the garbage with her pantyhose.

"OK, what do I do next?"

He produced a squirming, mud-encrusted worm from a tin can and held it out to her. "You gotta stick this on the hook."

"Uhh . . . well, since this is my first time, how about if you put the bait on the hook for me, all right?"

Mickey scraped some of the mud off the doomed worm with his fingernail, then speared it heartlessly onto the hook. He handed her the fishing pole.

"Oh, dear. That poor creature!"

"It's only a dumb worm. Now you have to cast it out in the river, like this." He demonstrated with an imaginary fishing pole. "Only make sure you don't let go of the pole."

Wilhelmina gripped the pole, drew her arm back like Mickey had shown her, then threw a perfect cast out into the middle of the river.

"That was fantastic! Are you sure you never fished before?"

"I'm positive. You must be a good teacher. What's next?"

"You just wait. If a fish starts to nibble on the worm, you'll feel a little tug and the bobber will go under."

"What's a bobber?"

161

"See that little red thing floating out . . . ? Hey! It's going down! You got a bite!"

"What?"

"Quick! Reel it in! Reel it in!"

"Oh, good heavens! Here, you do it, Mickey."

"No way! That's your fish, Professor. Just start turning the crank."

Wilhelmina's hands shook as she struggled to turn the reel. She could feel the resistance of the fish, fighting on the other end of the line. She cranked furiously. "How am I doing?"

"You've almost got it. You're doing great."

"Willymina? Mickey? Where are you?"

"Down here, Grandpa. Hurry up, the professor caught a fish." Mike scrambled down the bank and stopped beside her, panting slightly.

"Mike, take this thing, will you?"

"No way! I think it's against the law to catch fish in a state park." She stared at him, and his face split into a grin. "Grab the net there, Mickey, and wade out a little bit. Get ready to catch it. She's almost got it in now."

"There it is, Grandpa. I see it."

"Get the net under it."

Wilhelmina kept turning the crank as Mickey flailed around in the water. "I got it!" he cried at last and waved the net in triumph. A tiny fish, no more than six inches long, flopped around in it like a grasshopper. Mike laughed until the tears came.

"I've seen canned sardines bigger than that!"

"Oh, Mike, set the poor little thing free! It's only a baby."

"You're not supposed to feel sorry for the fish. How will we ever make a fisherman out of you?"

The words of Jesus sprang to Wilhelmina's mind as clearly as if they'd been spoken aloud. *Come, follow me, . . . and I will make you fishers of men.* But how should she begin? Surely fishing for men's souls wasn't as simple as fishing in a river.

"She felt sorry for the worm, too, Grandpa," Mickey said.

It was true. Wilhelmina had felt more pity for the fish and for a soulless worm than she had for Mike. She'd wanted nothing to do with him at first. Yet according to one of the verses on her 3" x 5" cards, God was not willing that any should perish.

O Lord, do it, she prayed. *Make me a fisher of men!*

"Well, so much for your first fishing adventure," Mike said, as he dropped the fish back into the river. "Hey, what happened to your sweater?"

Wilhelmina swallowed the lump of emotion in her throat. "I, uh . . . I had a little accident with the hook."

"I see." He bit his lip again. "Well, anyway, I found some matches, so we can start cooking supper if we want to."

"Supper! Oh dear. I told Larry I'd be back in time for the banquet."

"Well, I guess if we headed back right away I could have you home in a little over an hour."

Wilhelmina looked at her watch. "But by the time I

got changed and everything else it would be too late. Never mind. I suppose I can miss the banquet this year." She was amazed to discover how relieved she felt.

"You don't seem too broken up about it. What were they serving?"

"Prime rib."

"Well, I can beat that! Come on." He took her hand to help her up the riverbank. His palm was warm and rough from his work.

When they got to the top she could find only one shoe. "I wonder what happened to the other one?"

"Uh, oh. Buster! Get over here!" The dog romped up to Mike with Wilhelmina's soggy shoe dangling from his mouth. "Gimme that shoe, you stupid mutt!"

Buster wanted to play. He frolicked in front of them and refused to relinquish his hold on the shoe, no matter how loudly Mike yelled. Wilhelmina watched helplessly as the dog's teeth tore through the leather.

"Please, Buster. I need my shoe." Instantly, he dropped it in front of her. Mike scooped it up and slipped it, wet and slimy, back on her foot.

"Gosh, I'm really sorry about this, Willymina. I'd like to buy you a new pair."

"Don't be silly. They're only shoes."

Before long, Mike had a blazing fire lit. Wilhelmina sat beside him as he roasted a hot dog for her on a sharpened stick. When it was thoroughly charred, he folded a slice of bread around it and handed it to her.

"There now. Doesn't that beat a prime rib dinner?"

"Well, I don't know . . . but my dinner companions are certainly more entertaining."

They finished off the entire package of wieners. Wilhelmina couldn't remember when a hot dog had tasted so good. Mickey ate most of the potato chips and the dogs ate the stale donuts. Then they sat around the fire for more than an hour talking and laughing and listening to Mike sing crazy songs like "Bicycle Built for Two" and "Swanee River." He even convinced Wilhelmina and Mickey to join him in a round of "Row, Row, Row Your Boat" until they all dissolved into laughter. None of them noticed the darkening sky or the threatening storm clouds until the first few raindrops began to fall.

"We're going to get drenched!" Mike cried. "Mickey, you and the professor head back to the truck. I'll get your fishing gear and douse this fire. Hurry!"

Mickey dashed off and was soon well ahead of Wilhelmina. She stumbled down the trail in the deepening darkness, alone, trying not to imagine how many wild creatures were lurking behind the trees. The rain fell harder and faster. Twice, Buster and Heinz startled her half to death when they bounded back through the woods to look for her. After several minutes, she no longer cared about snakes or any other creatures. She simply longed for the promise of warmth from the truck's heater and shelter from the rain that streamed down in sheets.

By the time she reached the parking lot, Wilhelmina

was drenched. She climbed into the cab beside Mickey but before she could close the door, both dogs scrambled in with them.

"Oh, no! Bad dogs! Get out! *Out!*" she cried, but they refused to go back out into the rain. Their wet-dog smell overpowered her. As they trampled her lap with their muddy paws she wondered if her skirt would be salvageable or if it would be consigned to the garbage, as well.

When Mike finally sprinted out of the woods and opened the door of the truck, he took one look at the four, wet, miserable creatures huddling in the cab and burst out laughing.

It looked as if every light in Wilhelmina's house was lit when they pulled into her driveway. Her brother's car was parked near the garage. She looked at her watch. The Homecoming banquet must have ended earlier than usual. She said good night to Mike and Mickey, then crept through the back door, hoping to disappear quietly up the stairs and change her clothes before her brother noticed her.

But Larry was seated at the kitchen table with his head in his hands, still dressed in his suit and tie. Marjorie sat beside him, kneading a wadded up tissue. Her eyes were pink from weeping. Larry took one look at Wilhelmina and sprang to his feet.

"Good heavens! What happened to you? Have you been in an accident?"

She looked down at her clothes. Rainwater soaked

the front of Mike's scruffy bomber jacket and dripped from her stringy hair. Muddy paw prints and dog hair covered her skirt. A tail of yarn dangled from the jagged hole in her sweater as it slowly unraveled. A few tattered strings were all that remained of her pantyhose. Buster's teeth marks perforated her right shoe. She suppressed the urge to giggle at her brother's shocked expression.

"No, I'm fine, Larry."

"Well, where on earth have you been? We've been worried sick about you!"

"I'm sorry . . . I . . . I thought you'd be at the college. I never dreamed you'd be worried about me. Is the banquet over already?"

"We didn't go to the banquet."

"Well, that's silly. You could have gone without me—"

"Wilhelmina. The nursing home called right after you left. It's Father. He passed away."

9

Monday, October 19, 1987

When the 7:25 A.M. commuter flight to New York roared overhead, Mike knew he had overslept. He willed his body to get out of bed, but like the rusty Tin Man in *The Wizard of Oz*, his limbs refused to respond to his commands. He ached all over.

167

Buster and Heinz heard him stirring and bounded into the bedroom, tails thumping, fur shedding, tongues lolling in greeting.

"Yeah . . . yeah, I know, guys. I'm late today. You probably need to go out, right?" Buster woofed in reply.

Mike slowly sat up and swung his legs over the side of the bed. "I know I'm slowing down on you, guys, but this old body I'm trapped in is giving out on me. There's nothing I can do about it, either. I'm sorry, fellas." He patted Heinz on the head and gave Buster a quick scratch behind the ears. Then he shuffled to the back door in his bathrobe and slippers to let the dogs out.

He watched them from the kitchen window as they romped around the backyard with boundless energy, stopping to sniff at each new smell or to peer up into the treetops for squirrels. Mike could remember feeling that way once, young and full of energy, the world a new and exciting place every morning.

Deep in his heart Mike still felt that way. He still welcomed each day with a boundless zest for life. But his body, an aging Judas, had betrayed him.

In the distance, Mike heard a car door slam, and Buster and Heinz tore around to the side of the house, barking loudly. A moment later the front doorbell rang. Mike glanced at the kitchen clock. Who could it be at 20 minutes to 8 in the morning? He wasn't even dressed yet.

When he opened the front door, Steve, Cheryl, and

all three grandkids stood on his front porch. "Happy Birthday!" they shouted.

"I forgot what day it was!" Mike turned 66 today. He hadn't remembered.

Lori handed him a box of doughnuts as they piled into his living room. "Did you eat breakfast yet, Grandpa?"

"No, as a matter of fact, I didn't. Thank you."

"I'll put some coffee on, Dad," Cheryl said, kissing him on the cheek. "Happy birthday."

"Did we wake you up, Grandpa? You're still in your pajamas."

"No, Pete. I was already up . . . but, hey! Aren't you kids supposed to be in school today?"

"Yeah, Dad says we have to go right after we give you your birthday present," Mickey told him.

Steve flopped into Mike's tattered recliner and eased it back. "Cheryl's going to drive them later. I knew they'd never pay attention to their schoolwork if they didn't give you your present first thing this morning."

Mike held out both hands. "Well, let's have it, then. I love unwrapping presents."

For some reason Peter found this very amusing. He began to giggle. "It's not *here,* Grandpa. And it's not even wrapped because it's—"

Lori clapped her hand over Peter's mouth. "Be quiet! You're not supposed to tell! Daddy, make him be quiet. He's going to give it away."

Steve laughed as he brought the recliner upright again. "Better get dressed, Dad. These kids can't keep it secret much longer. Hey, Cheryl. Make that coffee to go."

When Mike was dressed they all piled into Steve's station wagon. The kids squirmed with excitement.

"You'll be so surprised, Grandpa."

"Not if you give it away, dummy."

"I sure hope this surprise is nearby," Mike said, "or I do believe one of these kids is going to burst like a balloon."

Steve drove the familiar route to the airfield and pulled up beside a small, vacant hangar not too far from their own.

"Close your eyes, Grandpa," Lori ordered. "And don't peek." Mike got out of the car and clamped his eyes shut. Peter and Lori took his hands and slowly led him into the hangar.

"OK, you can open them."

Steve switched on the overhead lights. "Ta da!"

A tattered airplane stood in the dimly lit hangar. It smelled like musty wood and castor oil. Mike gazed at it from end to end in disbelief.

"A Fokker DR-1 triplane?"

He walked slowly toward the plane, almost afraid the magnificent sight would disappear if he got too close. His eyes caressed every inch of it, from its sloping, down-turned tail, to its single, varnished wood propeller. He peered into the cramped, one-man open cockpit and stared up at the three tapering wings, piled one on top of the other.

"This is really mine?"

"Yep. Happy birthday, Dad."

"Maybe it was the Red Baron's plane," Peter said.

"Well, this was the kind of plane he flew, all right." Mike ran his hand over the faded, rotting fuselage, still unsure if he was dreaming. It was a genuine World War I vintage fighter plane. And it was his.

"Do you like it, Grandpa?" Lori asked.

"Honey, I love it! It's beautiful! I . . . I'm speechless!"

Steve laughed. "That's a first."

"Where on earth did you find this? I can't believe it." Mike hoped he wouldn't cry.

"It needs some work, as you can see," Steve said, poking his finger through the aging canvas. "But I figured it would give you something to do when you retire."

"Hey, are you trying to push me out to pasture?" Mike tried to frown, but he couldn't quite pull it off. He was unable to erase the look of awe and wonder on his face as he gazed at his new plane.

"You've worked hard all your life, Dad. You deserve a retirement hobby. But if I know you, you'll have this old relic airborne by springtime."

For a moment Mike had forgotten. He wouldn't live long enough to sit in the cockpit and fly this beautiful, marvelous antique. He ducked under the triple wings to hide his tears and busied himself near the tail section.

It wasn't fair. He didn't want to die. There were so many reasons to live, so much he still wanted to do.

But his son, Mike Jr., probably hadn't wanted to die either. He had been only 19 years old, with a girlfriend and a '54 Chevy waiting for him back home. And Helen hadn't wanted to die either. How she would have loved these grandkids of theirs. No, life wasn't always fair. But he had enjoyed a lot more of it than Mike Jr. and Helen had. He should be grateful.

"I'll help you paint it red, Grandpa," Lori said. "And we can put those cross-things on it like the Red Baron's plane."

"And I'll help you rebuild the engine," Mickey added. "Hey, check out this awesome landing gear."

"Maybe when you get the Fokker flying, Dad, I'll dig up a Sopwith Camel somewhere and we can have dogfights."

"And I'll whip your tail off!" Mike said as he swiped at his tears.

"Are you going to put a machine gun in it, Grandpa?" Peter asked.

Mickey scrambled up to examine the controls. "Yeah, where would the machine gun go, anyway?"

"It goes right up front there, so the Red Baron could fly and shoot at the same time," Mike said. "That was real flying. Man to man."

Mickey crawled into the cockpit and began firing an imaginary machine gun, complete with sound effects. "Wait a minute, Grandpa. How could he shoot without hitting his own prop?"

"That's a very good question." Mike stepped up on the lowest wing and pulled himself up beside Mickey.

"The earliest planes were hard to arm because of all the wires and struts in the way, not to mention the tail and the propeller blades. The pilots used to say, if you released a canary in the cockpit and he got away there must be an important wire missing."

"How'd they shoot, then?"

"Well, they didn't shoot at first. When World War I started, airplanes were such a new invention that they only thought to use them for aerial reconnaissance and artillery spotting. In fact, enemy pilots used to wave at each other as they flew by."

"No way!"

"Yep, that's the truth. Then one day a British pilot in a Bristol Scout fired a revolver at a German plane. The poor guy was so startled he landed and was taken prisoner. He became the first airman to ever be shot down. Then the arms race was on."

Petey scrambled up on the wing beside Mike. "Did they have bombs too?"

"You know what the first bombs were? Bricks! They just tossed bricks at each other. Bombs were too heavy. The planes couldn't get enough altitude with them on board. Or sometimes they'd throw out a grappling hook on a rope to try and grab the enemy plane's prop."

"But in the old movies I saw them firing machine guns during their dogfights," Mickey said.

"That's right, because sooner or later someone figured out a way to do it. A French stunt pilot invented the first interrupter gear so he could fire through his prop, but when his engine failed the Germans captured his plane. They hired Fokker, the guy who designed this triplane, to steal his idea. Fokker figured out how to synchronize the machine gun with the prop, and what followed was known as the 'Fokker scourge.' Once they solved the problem of shooting past their own prop, the Germans shot down so many planes that the Allied pilots were called 'Fokker fodder.' "

"The Red Baron was awesome!"

"Hey, whose side are you on, Mickey? But I'll admit, the Germans did have some fine pilots . . . Baron von Richthofen, Oswald Boelcke, Max Immelmann. They were real aces. In fact, both sides had some great heroes. They went up with no parachutes, little or no combat training, and sometimes barely enough flight training. They made up combat maneuvers as they went along."

"Why'd they make them up?"

"Well, new planes were being built and old ones redesigned so fast they didn't have time to test them properly. Sometimes just a small failure meant the pilot would be trapped in a disabled plane. There's the story of one poor fella who was trapped in a spinning plane with no escape and decided to end it all as quickly as he could. He gave the engine full throttle and dove straight toward the ground. Much to his surprise, the plane came out of it, and the pilot lived to tell about his new discovery—how to recover from a deadly spin."

"Grandpa, you know everything," Peter said.

Steve lifted Peter off the wing and set him down on the ground. "That's because Grandpa went to school. And so should you."

"What about Grandpa's birthday cake?" Lori asked.

"That's for supper. You'll see Grandpa then. Come on, now. Time to go." Cheryl herded them into the car.

"Bye, Grandpa. Happy birthday!"

After the kids left, Mike and Steve pored over every inch of the new plane together like two excited children.

"Look at this beautiful relic!"

"Do you think you can find all the parts you'll need, Dad?"

"What we can't find we'll improvise."

"All these wires and struts. They're something else!"

"Look at those three gorgeous wings, would you?"

"I like the square body design."

"And the tail! Look at the way it slopes."

"Not much room in this cockpit, is there?"

"You'll have to go on a diet, Steve, or you'll never fit."

"Pete said we should buy you a machine gun for Christmas."

"It could use a new paint job too."

"And a bath. It smells awful."

"It's the castor oil. They used it to lubricate the engines. Gosh, that smell brings back memories."

At last they locked up the hangar and walked the short distance across the tarmac to Dolan Aviation's cluttered office. Exhilarated, Mike could hardly get his mind back on the day's work. Steve was smiling, too, as he picked up the morning mail and paged through it.

"Hey, Dad . . . what's this?" his smile faded as he ripped open an envelope from Dr. Cole, the aviation medical examiner. "It's your flight physical renewal notice. Haven't you renewed this yet?"

Mike's flight of euphoria came to an abrupt crash. He hadn't renewed it because he knew he couldn't pass the required physical exam.

"You know what they say abut old age . . . the memory's the first thing to go . . . and I forget what's second."

"This is serious, Dad. You've only got, what . . . not even a week until the end of the month to renew it."

"Yeah, yeah, I'll do it."

"You had your physical already, right?"

"I told you, I went to the doc's a couple of weeks ago."

"Then let me run the personal information forms in this afternoon for him to sign. Otherwise you'll be grounded next Monday. Sunday will be the last day you can fly."

Mike grabbed the forms from Steve's hand. "Never mind. I'm going by there later today. I'll drop it off myself." He hated to lie to his son. But he hated the truth even more. Suddenly, he could no longer hold back his tears.

"Steve . . . I . . . I want to thank you again . . . for the plane—" Mike clasped his son in a fervent embrace.

10

Tuesday, October 20, 1987

The entire Faith Bible College community mourned the death of their former president and professor, Rev. Horatio Wesley Brewster. The administration canceled all classes. The college chapel was packed to capacity for the memorial service. But Wilhelmina couldn't mourn for her father. She had mourned for him months ago when his last stroke had separated them forever.

As the distinguished speakers delivered her father's eulogy, she felt no relief in knowing that he was finally at rest, restored and whole. It bothered her that he hadn't *died living* as Mike has phrased it. Instead, he'd languished slowly, dying bit by bit. It seemed like an unfair ending to such a fruitful, productive life, and she could almost understand Mike's desire to end his own life quickly before his dignity and usefulness eroded away.

She thought about her own life, the emptiness and vanity of her daily existence since her retirement. Could it even be called living? Her life was meaningless, serving no good purpose, yet Mike Dolan, who had so much to live for, so much vitality and zest for life, had to die. Why was God so unfair?

As she listened to the glowing words of praise for

177

her father, Wilhelmina sank deeper and deeper into depression. She hoped her friends would mistake it for grief.

When the funeral service ended, Wilhelmina's family, former colleagues, and friends gathered at her house. Mourners packed the living room and dining room, spilling over into the hallway and kitchen. Their somber faces, gloomy voices, and dark clothing depressed her even more. She wished they would all go home.

She made coffee in a daze. Piled the food provided by the church ladies onto serving platters. Poured tea. As she carried a tray full of dirty dishes to the kitchen, her brother Larry followed her, closing the door to the dining room behind them.

"Are you all right, Wilhelmina? You've hardly said a word to anyone all afternoon."

"I'm fine, Larry."

"Father wouldn't want us to mourn."

"Yes. I know."

She filled the sink with soapy water and busied herself with the dishes. She wished he'd leave. Instead, he stood frowning at her, playing with the watch chain that dangled across the front of his dark, three-piece suit. Another one of his sermons was imminent.

"It's your retirement, isn't it? That's what's really bothering you."

Go away. Just go away and leave me alone. She kept her hands underwater so he wouldn't see them trembling.

"Nothing's bothering me, Larry. I'm fine, considering that our father has just died." She hoped he'd mistake the quaver in her voice for grief.

"You've had since last spring to make plans and get yourself organized so you can enjoy your retirement. But all you've done is sit around and mope. Everyone's worried about you."

"Who says I have to *do* anything? It's *my* life! If I choose to sit around all day, what difference does it make?"

"You have too much talent to waste like this, Wilhelmina."

"Besides, I'm not just sitting around. I'm going to teach some private students."

"From the college?"

Wilhelmina remembered Lori's piano lesson, with Mrs. Treble Clef and Mr. Bass Clef, and blinked back her tears. "You'd never approve," she mumbled.

"What's that?"

"And I'm also working at the Cancer Center."

"Yes. Peter told me." He pulled out his watch and absently snapped the cover open and shut as if he had another appointment and she was wasting his time. "We thought you'd be on the board of directors. We had no idea the job would involve contact with the patients."

Wilhelmina slammed a cup into the drain board so hard she nearly broke it. "Cancer isn't contagious, Larry. And don't you and Peter have anything better to do than discuss my life?"

His face wore the pained look of a martyr. "This isn't like you, Wilhelmina. Peter and I are both concerned about you. We think you should pull yourself together." He snapped the watch open and shut again as if to emphasize his words. "What would Father say?"

"Father is dead. I can stop living my life to please him. And under no circumstances will I start living it to please you and Peter!" The look of shock on Larry's face was well worth the uncharacteristic outburst. She grabbed a towel to dry her hands and stalked into the dining room.

The scene there hadn't changed. She busied herself at the food table, rearranging the platters, moving the sugar bowl closer to the coffeepot, lining up the silverware in neat little rows. She had the uncomfortable feeling that she was being watched. She looked up. Her brother Peter and Dean Bradford were glancing furtively at her while they talked. She picked up a plate with an entire chocolate layer cake and marched over to them.

"Here. Have some cake, Dean Bradford." She shoved the plate into his hands. His eyes grew wide. "Peter, could I see you for a minute, please?" She grabbed Peter's arm and propelled him into the kitchen with her.

"Now, Mina, don't overreact . . ." He tried his charming, politician's smile on her, but it froze under her icy glare.

"You have no right to interfere, Peter. I told you not to go begging for my job."

"I wasn't begging. We were just discussing some possibilities, that's all."

"You have no right to do that! Maybe I don't want my job back. Did that ever occur to you?"

"That college was your life, Mina. Larry and I both know it, so don't try to tell us otherwise. And after everything Father did for that school, they owe us a small favor or two."

Angry tears sprang into Wilhelmina's eyes against her will. "I don't want my job back for Father's sake, don't you understand? If Dean Bradford asks me back, I want it to be because of *me*. Because of what *I* have to offer. Do you get it, Peter? Mind your own business!"

Two explosions in one day. After a lifetime of abstinence. What was happening to her? She stalked from the kitchen for the second time, leaving another stunned brother behind. They would certainly have a lot to talk about now. "We were only trying to help." . . . "Poor Wilhelmina." She didn't want their pity, she wanted their respect. But evidently she'd lost that when she'd lost her job.

Back in her living room, people milled around, talking and eating, showing no signs of going home. She felt like a stranger in her own house. She wished this day was over. She was tired of being polite to everyone.

"Wilhelmina . . ."

Someone touched her shoulder. She turned around. Catherine Hall looked into Wilhelmina's eyes and, it seemed, into her heart. "I understand," Catherine said simply.

And Wilhelmina knew that of all the people gathered there, Catherine really did understand her loss. Eight years ago, after a lifetime on the mission field with her husband, John, Catherine had lost everything in a political uprising. The mission station, field hospital, and church had all burned to the ground. Her husband had been tortured and killed. Wilhelmina's problems abruptly shrank into proportion.

"Your father was a very great man, Mina. You must be very proud of him. He has earned a hero's welcome into the courts of heaven. 'Well done, good and faithful servant.'"

Catherine was the only person who had spoken of Wilhelmina's father with joy instead of in morbid tones of sorrow. No one else seemed to believe that heaven was paradise or that an 89-year-old man might be glad to leave the suffocating confines of a nursing home to live there.

"Thank you, Catherine." It was all she could manage to say.

"John and I both owed so much to your father. It was because of his preaching that we went to the mission field. He challenged us with the words of Christ: 'Whoever finds his life will lose it, and whoever loses his life for my sake will find it.'"

John had been one of Father's most brilliant students, a man who could have easily earned degrees and titles and a prestigious position within the denom-

182

ination. But he had chosen to lay it all aside to work in a backward, unstable third-world country. Wilhelmina had always thought of John's decision to become a missionary as a terrible waste. Today, for the first time, she wondered if she had been wrong.

"John thanked God for your father's inspiration and encouragement every day of his life. I often wished your father could have traveled to all the places where he sent his missionaries and seen the millions of lives that were changed because of him."

Wilhelmina longed to confide in Catherine.

"Let's go someplace where we can talk," she whispered.

They waded through the crowded rooms to the kitchen. Thankfully, it was empty. Wilhelmina plunged her hands into the tepid dishwater and began to wash, struggling for a place to begin. How should she describe her own empty life, the feeling that she'd also lost everything? Catherine picked up a dish towel and began to dry, waiting patiently.

"Catherine . . . how did you ever get through it all? I mean, when you lost John, and everything you had worked for all your life . . . how . . . ?" Tears cut her question short.

Catherine finished drying a cup and set it on the counter. "When I felt bitter and defeated and ready to give up, your father ministered to me. He found me . . . I don't even know how . . . but he showed up on my doorstep one day in Boston when I was so depressed I could barely function. For a long time he didn't say a word, he just held me and cried with me. Then he told me that your mother had cancer and was probably going to die, and he talked about his own failing health. He told me, 'We have two choices, you and I; we can lose ourselves in despair or find ourselves in Christ.'"

"He reminded me of the disciples, James and John, who wanted a position of greatness in Christ's kingdom. 'Can you drink the cup I am going to drink?' Jesus asked them. Your father said that everything that had happened to me on the mission field and everything that was happening in his life was part of that cup. We needn't feel ashamed for shrinking back from its bitter taste. Even Jesus prayed, 'If it is possible, may this cup be taken from me.' But in the end Jesus prayed, 'My Father, if it is not possible for this cup to be taken away unless I drink it, may your will be done.'

"Then your father asked me, 'Is the servant greater than his Master? Shouldn't you and I also willingly . . . *willingly* . . . suffer the loss of all things?'"

Wilhelmina remembered her father's final year of life. He had gradually lost everything—his mobility, his speech, his capacity to think and reason, his dignity. But he had been willing to lose it all for Christ's sake, without needing to know why. Wilhelmina knew that she had been wrong about him. Father *had* died 'living.' She let Catherine take her in her arms and allowed her tears to flow.

"Everything changed for me after that day with your

184

father," Catherine told her. "Now I find myself doing things that I never dreamed I could have done. But first I had to stop shaking my fist at God and asking *why*. Instead I decided to say *yes* to His will for my life, no matter what that meant."

Wilhelmina dried her tears and looked once again into her friend's eyes. "Catherine, I've been very angry at God. I want to say *yes*, but . . . but I think God is asking me to do something . . . to minister to someone . . . and I don't know how. How do you tell someone about Christ? How do you bridge the gap when there are . . . cultural differences? What do you say?"

Catherine picked up another cup and slowly dried it, pondering the question as if unwilling to give a pat answer. When she finally replied, there were tears in her eyes.

"Before you ever preach a word to them, Mina . . . before you even open your mouth to speak, get down on your knees and ask God to help you love that person. Christ didn't save the world with His words, did He? He saved it with His love. Do you love this person? Really love him?"

Wilhelmina didn't answer. She didn't know. She watched as Catherine's tears overflowed and spilled down her cheeks. "We were warned to leave the mission station, that there was trouble coming. But John refused to go. He sent me to safety, but he insisted on staying with the tribespeople. He loved them. He was a very gifted preacher. Knowledgeable. Articulate.

Persuasive. But more people came to Christ after John's death than all during his lifetime. Because 'greater love has no one than this, that he lay down his life for his friends.' He may not hear your words, Mina. But he'll see Christ in your love."

Late that afternoon, when everyone had finally gone home, Wilhelmina drove out to the cemetery alone. The day had been gray and cold and as she walked to her father's grave, pulling the belt of her raincoat tighter around her, the bitter wind whispered that winter was on its way.

The canopy, railing, and chairs were gone, and the earth around her father's grave looked ugly and scarred, mounded high as if an ordinary grave couldn't contain him. The funeral wreaths had begun to wilt in the chilly air, and dry brown leaves swirled across the bare earth. The leafless tree branches scraped against each other in the wind.

Beside his grave, her mother's was grassy and smooth. That wound, like Wilhelmina's sorrow, had healed over time. The pain she now felt would also heal. Like the seasons, life was ever-changing. Only God remained forever the same.

She remembered reading about the Jewish custom of placing a small stone on the headstone after visiting a grave and bent down to place one on her parents' tombstone.

Wilhelmina walked back to her car, then drove to the tiny building that housed the cemetery offices. A large woman in a garishly printed orange dress slouched in a chair behind the counter, reading a tabloid.

"Excuse me. Do you have a book or something that would tell me if a person is buried here?" Wilhelmina asked.

The woman waved her cigarette at a shelf of ledger books. "It's all up there. Alphabetical. Help yourself."

Wilhelmina scanned the untidy shelves, paging through three ledger books before she found what she was searching for. She asked for directions to "The Garden of Tranquillity," then drove through the cemetery to a quiet, older site near the back.

The two graves were well cared for. Rust-colored mums, wilted by the cold fall weather, grew in large pots on each grave. A bronze U.S. Air Force plaque marked the foot of one grave. A small, faded American flag flapped in the breeze. *Cpl. Michael G. Dolan, Jr., U.S.A.F.,* the headstone read. *March 1, 1948—Sept. 23, 1967.* He had been only 19 years old.

To the right of Michael's grave was his mother's. *Helen Ann Dolan.* Again Wilhelmina subtracted the dates. Mike's wife had died at the age of 48.

What had she been like? Wilhelmina knew nothing about her except that she had played the piano and had attended church, taking her two sons with her. Her tombstone was centered over a double plot. The grave beside Helen's was empty.

As Wilhelmina looked around at the barren tree branches, the dry, brown grass, the withered flowers, a desperate sense of urgency gripped her. She stooped to pick up two small stones and placed one on each grave marker, praying that God would help her before it was too late.

11

Saturday, October 24, 1987

A blaring car horn woke Wilhelmina from a dreamless sleep. Exhausted from the funeral a few days ago, she had fallen asleep on her sofa, watching the evening news. Was the car horn on TV? She gazed, bleary-eyed at her grandmother's clock on the mantelpiece. Almost 6:30.

She yawned and sat up to hear the weather report. Her neck ached from the cramped sleeping position. The horn tooted again. It sounded as if the car was in her driveway. What day was it? Friday? No, Saturday. Was she supposed to be somewhere tonight? Her doorbell rang.

With a vague feeling of dread, Wilhelmina smoothed her clothes and hurried to open the front door. Mike Dolan stood on her doorstep.

It had only been a week since she'd gone fishing with him, but Wilhelmina was shocked by how thin and unwell he looked. His skin was faintly yellow, like old sheet music. But his broad smile was unchanged.

"Evening, Ma'am. I hope I'm not disturbing you."

"Well, no . . . not really. I was just watching TV."

"I suppose this is kind of short notice again, but it's a beautiful Indian summer evening, and I was hoping you could come along and help us out."

"Help who? With what?"

Mike grinned. "Why don't you grab a jacket and find out. It'll be a surprise. Have you had supper? We've got some doughnuts and a jug of coffee in the truck."

Wilhelmina gazed at him mutely as she tried to sort everything out. She couldn't eat doughnuts. She hated surprises. And she'd hoped she'd never have to ride in Mike's rusted pickup truck again. What she really wanted was to go back inside and watch TV. But she also wanted to say *yes* to God.

"All right, come in. I'll get ready."

"No, I'll wait out here. My grandson Pete's in the truck."

As she hurried upstairs to comb her hair and grab a sweater, Wilhelmina began to have second thoughts. She didn't even know where she was going. She welcomed the chance to talk to Mike, but how much would she be able to say with Mike's little grandson listening. She certainly couldn't mention Mike's illness or discuss why suicide was wrong. Perhaps she shouldn't have agreed to go. She looked at herself in the mirror as she combed her hair, certain that she was looking at a fool.

Mike helped her climb in the passenger's seat, then

ran around and slid behind the wheel. Peter sat between them, clutching a box of doughnuts. He had blobs of sticky red jam on his face, a fine dusting of powdered sugar down the front of his sweatshirt, and a mouthful of doughnuts.

"There's still some jelly ones left," he told her. "They're my favorites."

"So I see. Maybe later."

As they drove across town, most of the traffic seemed to be young people, cruising the streets on a Saturday night. But dozens of cars poured through the main gates of the city park and Mike followed them inside. A large sign announced "The Eighth Annual Fall Hot Air Balloon Race." Arrows directed spectators to the right, participants to the left. Mike turned left.

"Oh, Mike! You can't be serious!"

"It'll be great. You'll love it." Peter bounced up and down on the seat with excitement.

It was the same field where the kite contest had been held, but this time dozens of pickup trucks and vans were parked along the edge. Work crews scurried around, unloading gondolas, fans, and all sorts of strange equipment. Mike parked the truck and turned off the engine.

"There's Max over there," he said. "Let's go."

"Can't I stay here and watch? I don't know a thing about this."

"Hey, I was serious about Max needing our help. We're his pit crew, so you can't back out now. He won't get very far without us."

Wilhelmina hauled herself out of the truck and trudged across the grass behind Mike and Peter. She saw two local TV stations setting up camera crews and wondered if the entire city was about to watch her make a fool of herself again.

Max was a stocky, bulldog of a man in his mid-60s with an unlit cigar sticking out of his mouth. If he had been an actor, he could have easily played the part of Winston Churchill.

"Max, I'd like you to meet your new pit crew member, Willymina Brewster. This is my old air force buddy, Maxwell Barker. He'll tell us what we need to do."

Max scrutinized Wilhelmina as if deciding whether or not she would measure up. "Brewster, huh? You any relation to Brewster Hall and Brewster Library and all them other Brewsters over at the college?" Wilhelmina nodded. He gave an ambiguous grunt and jerked his thumb toward the back of his truck. "Let's get her unloaded."

They obviously expected Wilhelmina to help, so she went to work, helping to lower a wicker gondola from Max's pickup. It felt amazingly flimsy to her—little more than an overgrown laundry basket. Strapped inside, looking oddly out of place, was a fire extinguisher. They set the gondola on the ground, then Max tossed an array of other equipment down to them, which they spread out beside the basket. All along the field on either side of them, about two dozen other crews were going through the same routine. Max tossed Mike a long bag.

"Here, help me get this burner set up."

He jumped down from the truck and handed Wilhelmina one end of a thick rope. The other end was tied to the gondola.

"Can you tie a knot, Miz Brewster? Tie this onto the truck bumper. Tight enough to hold it, but loose enough to get it off in a hurry."

The responsibility overwhelmed her. She had visions of the knot coming loose prematurely and the balloon taking off with no one in it. Or worse, sailing away with the truck still attached like the tail of a kite because she'd tied the knot too tightly. She looked at Max helplessly, but he was busy helping Mike assemble the stand to the propane burner. Peter was trying to lug the nylon balloon out of a huge bag.

Tight enough to hold, loose enough to get off in a hurry . . . , she murmured to herself as she fumbled with the rope.

"Let's give Pete a hand with the balloon," Mike shouted to her when she'd finished with what she hoped was a satisfactory knot.

She grabbed a handful of nylon and started pulling the multicolored balloon out of the bag and spreading it on the field. But the more she pulled out, the more of it there seemed to be. It kept emerging, unfurling endlessly from the bag.

"Why, it's enormous! There must be thousands of

yards of it! I never dreamed it was so huge!" She was truly astounded at its size.

"Yeah, I think this thing could cover my whole house," Mike said. "We've got to spread it out all the way. The end with the cables attaches to the gondola, so make sure it's down here. There are shroud lines on top that should be spread out too."

Wilhelmina glanced over at the other balloonists who were spreading their balloons across the grass as well. "Is this really a race? Where's the finish line?"

"It's a race, all right, but the finish line is wherever the wind takes us. They'll send up a chase balloon first, and it'll drop a marker out in the country somewhere. We have to try to get airborne soon afterward—before the wind changes direction—and follow it. Then we'll drop our flag as close to the marker as we can. The closest flag wins."

Wilhelmina's stomach turned queasy every time Mike said *we*. She continued to tug on the balloon, spreading it out across the grass, and it continued to grow, larger and larger every minute. At last the bag was empty and a huge sea of nylon, covered with multicolored stripes, lay before her. Max tipped the gondola on its side and attached the balloon cables to it. Now the entire field seemed to be blanketed with brightly colored nylon cloth, the various shaped gondolas tipped over and waiting. A small shiver of excitement raced through her.

A loudspeaker announcement called for all pilots to report to the officials' booth for a short meeting. Max wiped his greasy hands on the seat of his trousers and strode away, the unlit cigar still clamped tightly between his teeth.

"Things are going to get real exciting in a minute," Mike warned her. He plugged two large fans into a portable generator, then started the generator. "When Max gets back, we're each going to have a job to do. Pete, you hold the balloon's mouth wide open, like this, see? Willymina, when Max says so, you're going to start up these fans and make sure they're aimed inside the balloon."

"Oh, Mike . . . I can't—"

He ignored her protest and pointed to the top of the balloon, halfway across the field. "I'll be down there, hanging on to the shroud ropes so we don't float away before we're ready."

"But, Mike . . . I never—"

"When Max gets ready to fire the burner, make sure you're both out of the way. That burner is hot!"

"Mike, listen—"

"Oh, and don't forget to plug your ears. The burner makes a real racket. Get ready, here he comes."

The pilots hurried back from their meeting, with Max in the lead, still chomping on his dead cigar.

"There goes the chase balloon, Grandpa."

Wilhelmina looked up as a brilliant blue balloon lifted off and slowly floated above them.

"Get ready," Mike said. He sprinted across the colorful sea of nylon to hold down the shroud ropes on top.

"Start the fans, Miz Brewster," Max shouted above the roar of the generator. He helped Peter hold the mouth of the balloon open while Wilhelmina fumbled for the fan switch. The first one started up with a rumble and nearly vibrated out of her grip as she tried to aim it toward the opening.

"OK. Now the other one," Max yelled.

The second fan started with a jerk and she struggled to aim it into the slowly swelling balloon. Peter looked as if his clothes were about to be blown off in the wind. He laughed so hard he could barely stand up. Max crawled inside the huge balloon and unfurled it from within, making sure the air from the fans reached every empty space.

Slowly, magnificently, like a huge, prehistoric monster, the balloon came to life, swelling up in front of Wilhelmina, looming larger every second. All around her, dozens of brilliantly colored balloons were rising up as if God suddenly declared, "Let there be life," and the living creatures arose from the dust of the earth. A glorious thrill of excitement coursed through her veins at the breathtaking sight.

"Get out of the way," Max shouted as he sprinted past her. "I'm going to fire the burner."

She motioned to Peter, and they both stepped aside. But she forgot to plug her ears and the sudden, deafening roar of the burner caused her to clutch at her heart, which had momentarily ceased to beat. The intense heat from the burner made her take a few steps back.

Slowly, ponderously, the top of the balloon began to rise as the air inside it warmed. It swung around to a vertical position, pulling the gondola upright along with it. She saw Mike, hanging onto the shroud lines, guiding the balloon so it would rise up smoothly. It was a magnificent spectacle, as graceful and beautiful as a ballet.

"Get in! Get in!" Max shouted. He was talking to her. "Hurry up, Miz Brewster!"

"No . . . I . . . I can't!"

"I need a spotter," he shouted. "Get in!"

Deep in her heart, Wilhelmina longed to go. But she stood rooted to the ground, unable to move. Mike sprinted up beside her and tugged on her arm.

"Come on, get in, Professor. You'll love it once you're up there." The gondola lifted from the ground a few inches, but it was still tied to the truck bumper by Wilhelmina's knot.

"I can't . . . I just can't." She couldn't will her feet to move.

"Somebody better get in, *fast!*" Max shouted. Several other balloons had already lifted off and were slowly floating skyward.

"You go, Mike. I can't." He studied her for a moment and seemed to understand her tremendous fear.

"OK, Professor," he said gently. "Untie the rope."

He ran to the gondola and hoisted himself over the side while Wilhelmina undid her knot. Max fired the burner again and the flame shot up with a deafening *whoosh.* The balloon seemed to draw a deep breath. For a moment it didn't move, then the gondola rocked slightly and began to bump across the ground.

"Max, wait a minute!" Mike shouted as the balloon bounced slowly away from her. "I forgot to tell her what to do!"

"I can't stop now!" The balloon rose a few more feet.

"Willymina, listen! You gotta follow us in the chase car!"

"What?" She could barely hear him above the roar of the burners. She jogged across the field behind them as the balloon drifted slowly skyward.

He cupped his hands around his mouth and shouted down to her. "Follow us in my truck!" The giant balloon rose above her head as if by levitation and floated away from her. She sprinted faster to keep up.

"I can't drive your truck!" she panted.

"Willymina you have to! We need you to pick us up!"

"But . . . but . . ."

"Here, catch!" He tossed the keys down to her from the balloon and they landed in the grass about 10 feet in front of her. Then, like a huge, magical sailing ship, the balloon suddenly caught a breeze and floated off into the clear, evening sky. Multicolored balloons filled the heavens, and Wilhelmina paused to catch her breath, watching in awe as they drifted slowly away. She would never forget the magnificent sight.

She was still gazing at the sky when she felt

someone tugging on her sleeve. Peter held Mike's keys out to her.

"We're gonna lose them," he said.

"What? Aren't those his keys?"

"No, Grandpa's balloon. We have to hurry up and follow them."

"Do we have to leave right now?"

"How else are we going to know where they land?" he said, giggling.

It took Wilhelmina a moment to realize what Peter was telling her. She glanced anxiously back up at the sky, searching for Mike's balloon. It sailed high above the trees, moving away at an alarming rate of speed. She grabbed Peter's arm and hurried toward the truck.

"You forgot the bag," Peter told her when they reached the parking lot.

"What bag?" she said, panting.

"The bag that the balloon goes in. We're supposed to bring it with us."

Wilhelmina groaned and hurried back to retrieve the huge canvas bag, lugging it clumsily behind her. She could barely catch her breath. She hadn't exhausted this much energy in her life. She glanced up at the sky once again. The balloons were rapidly sailing northeast.

She fumbled the keys into the ignition but forgot to put the clutch in. The truck lurched forward and stalled, nearly slamming Peter into the dashboard. Some loose change and an envelope slid onto the floor.

"I'm sorry. I haven't driven a standard shift in ages. You'd better buckle up." She restarted the engine and lurched, kangaroo-like, out of the parking lot and through the gates. Peter picked up the envelope and pulled out its contents. She glanced at the letterhead: "Aviation Medical Examiner."

"What is that, Peter? It looks important. You'd better put it back."

"I know how to read, wanna hear me?" He read haltingly, sounding out each word. "De-ar . . . Mis-ter . . . Do-lan. Your . . . Avi-a-tion . . . Med-i-cal . . . what's this word?"

"Certificate."

"Certificate . . . is . . . due . . . to . . . ex-pi-re . . . on . . . the . . . last . . . day . . . of . . . this . . . month . . ."

"Peter, not now. Please. I need you to help me find the balloon."

He stuffed the letter back into the envelope and peered out of the windshield. Wilhelmina negotiated the truck through the traffic, hopping and lurching comically as she struggled with the clutch.

"I don't see them no more," he told her.

"*Any* more—What! You don't see them?"

"Nope. I dunno where they all went."

"Well, maybe we'll see them again after I cross the bridge. I'm going in the wrong direction at the moment, but it's the only way to get across the river."

"We probably shoulda brought the walkie-talkie."

"There's a walkie-talkie?"

"Uh-huh. Uncle Max . . . well, he's not really my

uncle but that's what we call him . . . Uncle Max always carries a walkie-talkie in his balloon so he can talk to us and—"

"Oh, Peter! Where's our walkie-talkie?"

Peter grinned, revealing a gap where his two front teeth were missing. "I dunno. Probably still in Uncle Max's truck."

"Of course. Well, we're not going back for it now. We'll just have to follow along as best we can. Keep watching the sky."

Peter peered intently through the windshield for a few minutes, then seemed to grow bored, squirming in his seat.

Suddenly she spotted a splash of color against the sky. "Peter, look! There they are!"

"We found them! And I see Grandpa's balloon too."

"Yes, now let's make sure we keep them in sight this time."

Peter squirmed restlessly on the seat. "Um . . . Professor Brewster?"

"What is it, Peter?"

"I have to go to the bathroom."

The people and cars in the park below Mike grew smaller and smaller as the balloon carried him silently upward. They crossed the river, a winding strip of gray steel, and sailed over the twinkling city.

"I sure hope your lady friend has sense enough to follow us," Max said. "I don't feel much like sitting in a cow pasture all night."

"She'll come."

"Then why was she just standing there after we took off?"

"I think she was in shock. She's never done stuff like this before. She's spent her whole life in school-rooms and concert halls."

"Sounds thrilling."

"Yeah, I know what you mean." Mike leaned against the side of the cramped basket and looked down at the city as it slowly passed below them.

"I thought we could get her on board if we didn't give her too much time to think about it. But she was terrified. She shook like a willow in a windstorm. I'm sorry, Max."

"I'll forgive you . . . providing she ever finds us again. Do you suppose she had enough sense to bring along the walkie-talkie?" He picked up his receiver and switched it on. They listened to the hissing static.

"Pete might think to remind her. Then again, he might not."

"This is the last time I let *you* pick our pit crew."

Mike's smile faded as the irony of Max's words struck him. He turned away to gaze down at the passing countryside: rolling hills and fence rows; miniature houses and barns; scattered clumps of leaf-less trees.

Tomorrow.

Mike had to take his final flight tomorrow. After that, his pilot's license would no longer be valid. He wasn't afraid but deeply saddened. His life was over.

He had reached the end of it at last. Why did he feel like he had just begun to live?

"Do you see that chase balloon anywhere?" Max asked.

"Yep, I see it. Up ahead of us."

Max fired the burners for about 10 seconds, and Mike felt the heat on the top of his head. Then everything fell silent again. He could even hear the sound of voices on the ground below him, and he watched the movement of tiny people and cars, scurrying about. The evening air smelled clean and pure as it gently brushed his face.

It felt odd to be flying through the clear, evening sky with no Plexiglas windshield, no humming engines, no tachometer or air speed indicator to watch. Unlike an airplane, balloon flight offered tremendous freedom. Max had no gauges and dials to watch, no controls or ailerons to worry about, no need to even file a flight plan. In fact, there was very little Max could do to control which direction they went or even where they would land. Mike envied Max's liberty. Maybe this random, uncontrolled journey, harnessed to a giant bubble of warm air, was really the purest form of flight.

"You're looking kind of thin these days, Mike. You been feeling all right?"

"Yeah, I've been on a diet. I needed to lose some weight."

"Well, it's none of my business, but I think you overdid it. You lost a little too much."

202

"You're as bad as Steve. He's jealous too. Hey, it's none of my business, but I thought you quit smoking?"

"The cigar ain't lit, is it?"

"Not at the moment, but don't you find it tempting to have it hanging out of your mouth all the time like that?"

"You got a match, Mike?"

He checked his pockets. "No."

"Well, I ain't got one either. I decided you don't quit smoking by not buying cigars. The best way to quit is to stop buying matches!" They both laughed. Mike turned around to look behind them.

"Well, what do you know. That looks like my truck down there, Max. Only one headlight."

"Yeah, well she's driving it down a dead-end road."

"You and I can see that, but she can't. At least she's following us."

"What's with you and this Brewster lady? New girlfriend?"

"No, just a friend."

"Then you won't mind me saying she's awful homely."

"She's got a different kind of beauty, Max," Mike said quietly. "And she's a mighty fine piano player too. But she's one of the unhappiest people I've ever met. Rarely smiles, always stern, you know what I mean? She's got plenty of money, but I don't think she's ever had a day of fun in her life. I read in the paper that her father died recently, so I thought I'd cheer her up, give her a chance to live it up a little in your balloon. But she was just too scared to try."

Mike watched as his tiny truck reached the end of the dirt road and stopped. He turned to face Max. "I can't figure people like her out. I mean, what good is it to live on this beautiful earth if all you do is eat and sleep and work and die? Life is for living, taking risks, trying something new."

"Yeah, I agree. But there's an awful lot of people who live their whole lives in the same rut. Too scared to climb out and live for a change."

"I know, and it's a shame. Why can't people stop being afraid of their mortality and take a few chances. There's nothing any of us can do to hang on to our lives anyway, so we may as well die living."

Max grunted and gestured with his soggy cigar. "You're getting to be a real philosopher. I'll have them put that on your tombstone. 'He died living.'"

Mike met his friend's gaze. "I'd appreciate that, old buddy," he said quietly.

Below him, Wilhelmina had turned the truck around and was speeding back toward a main road. Then a sudden movement on the horizon caught Mike's eye. The bright blue balloon dipped down behind a hill, momentarily out of sight, then soared up once again.

"Look! The chase balloon's going down. I'll bet it's making the drop."

"It's a good thing you're sharp, Mike. They dropped that so fast, if you'd have blinked you'd have missed it. I'll tell you something, that guy's an excellent balloonist!"

"And so are you, my friend. He dropped it right behind that hill over there. Let's win this thing!"

With the precision of an expert, Max fired the burner just long enough to give them lift and momentum. Then he let the wind carry them to where the chase balloon had made the drop. When they got beyond the hill, Mike scanned the ground until he spotted the large, florescent-orange marker.

"There it is, Max. And you're headed right for it."

"Quick, where's our flag?"

"I thought you had it."

Max nearly bit his cigar in half. "You mean we forgot the blasted flag?"

Mike laughed as he pulled the weighted flag out from behind his back and waved it at Max.

"What the blazes are you trying to do, Mike, give me a heart attack or something? Give me that thing!"

"You mind your burners and get us down there without crashing. I'll drop it over the side. Tell me when."

Max guided the balloon down as low as he dared to go without landing. Mike leaned over the side, dropping the flag within inches of the marker. As Max fired the burners to ascend again, they cheered.

"I'd like to see some joker beat that," Max said. "This calls for a cigar."

"I thought you were out of matches?"

"Maybe I can light it on the burner." They laughed uproariously.

As they sailed effortlessly into the darkening sky,

Mike felt at peace. "You know, Max, I'm glad I got the chance to come with you, after all. Look at that sky. Isn't it a gorgeous night? This has been a fantastic flight."

"Yeah, I hate to see it end, but I'm almost out of fuel. We need to look for a place to land where there's nothing growing. I just hope your friend can find us in the dark."

"Well, if she doesn't see us, I'll bet she can hear us. We've been laughing like a couple of hyenas."

"Look, there's a perfect spot. Hang on and I'll try to put us down over there. By the way, I'm not famous for my smooth landings."

"I teach flying lessons, remember? I know all about rough landings."

"Hang on, then. I'm gonna let the air out."

Max pulled a rip cord that detached an entire panel of nylon near the top of the balloon. The giant bag began to collapse as the air rushed out of it. The decision to land was irreversible. The ground rapidly rose up toward them. The gondola bounced once or twice, then landed with a jolt, tipping over on its side. Mike and Max tumbled out on top of each other, a tangled pile of arms and legs. The deflated balloon drifted gracefully to the ground beside them.

"You all right, Mike?"

"Yeah, how about you? I think I kicked you in the head."

"I'm fine. Good thing it was you, though. I don't think that Brewster lady would've appreciated landing on top of me. This field is bumpier than it looked from up there."

"Every runway in the world looks smooth until you land on it. Hey, here comes my one-eyed truck. She did a pretty good job of chasing us, for her first time at it, don't you think?"

"Yeah, but after today . . . leaving her stranded in the middle of the park like we did . . . do you really think you can talk her into a second time?"

12

Wilhelmina was extremely distressed to learn that they had won first place in the balloon race. She stood grimly between Mike and Max, who was still chomping on his cigar, as the two men raised champagne glasses. Flashbulbs blinded her. Minicams whirred. Her picture would be in all the morning newspapers, and since tomorrow was Sunday, it would probably be posted on the church bulletin board again. How would she ever survive the notoriety? If her friends thought a kite contest was disgraceful, what on earth would they think of this?

By the time the trophies were awarded, the victory speeches given, and the celebrating finished, it was nearly eleven o'clock. Little Peter could barely keep his eyes open.

"Do you mind if I drop him off first, Professor? He's tuckered out."

"I'm not in a hurry." Within minutes, Peter was asleep in the truck with his sweaty head nestled on Wilhelmina's lap. Mike glanced over at them and smiled.

"This was the third time now that I've run off and left you with one of my grandkids. I'm sorry, Willymina."

She smiled to herself as she thought of her day at the ballet with Lori, fishing with Mickey, and now chasing a balloon all over the countryside with Peter.

"You know, I've never had much patience with children, but yours are really . . . rather special. Peter reminds me a lot of my younger brother at that age."

Mike pulled the truck to a stop. "We're home, Pete. Say good night to Professor Brewster."

Peter sat up and looked around, blinking sleepily. Then he wrapped his arms around Wilhelmina's neck and hugged her. She blinked back her sudden tears. "Good night, Peter," she murmured. Then added something her own mother always said, "Sweet dreams."

When Mike returned to the truck, Wilhelmina's heart began to race. The time had come. She was finally alone with him. What should she say? How should she begin?

"I hope you had a good time tonight, Willymina."

"Oh, I did! I really did!"

"Next time you'll have to go up for a ride, though. It's a fantastic experience."

"I'm really sorry about that, Mike. I should have gone, but . . . I don't know . . . I guess I froze."

"I know the feeling. That happened to me the first time I had to make a parachute jump. I got as far as the open door of the plane, looked down . . . and froze. My first mistake was to look down, of course. Never look down before you jump!"

"So what happened? Did you finally get up your nerve to jump?"

"Nope. Never had to. My C.O. booted me in the rear end and pushed me out. What a feeling, falling out of that airplane the first time! I never will forget that. I thought my life was over."

"But your parachute opened, didn't it?"

"Sure it did. They attach the rip cords to the plane so it opens as soon as you jump . . . or get pushed. They don't take a chance that you'll faint or forget to pull it yourself."

Wilhelmina shivered. For a moment she envied his many experiences, his sense of adventure. "What's it like to parachute?"

"Once you get past the open door it's fantastic! You fall through the air for what seems like a year, but it's really only a few seconds, then there's a whoosh and the chute opens. It pulls you up in the air, like you're a marionette and God's got a hold of the strings. After that, you can relax and enjoy the ride."

When Mike mentioned God, Wilhelmina saw her opening. She felt like she was standing before the open door of the airplane, trying to muster her courage. She drew a deep breath and jumped in clumsily.

"Do you believe in God, Mike?"

"Sure I do. I'd have to be blind not to."

"Are you a Christian?"

"I never could figure out how to answer that. I was brought up going to church—went to Sunday School every week with my mother. All of us kids did. So, I always figured I was a Christian. Then one time during the war I was sitting around with the guys getting ready to go out on a mission over Germany escorting a bomber formation . . . an awful lot of planes had been shot down before us, you know? Well anyhow, me and another pilot started talking. He asked me if I was a Christian. I said, yeah, I go to church. He said that wasn't enough. Going to church didn't make you a Christian. Wouldn't you know it, I got hit that time out and my plane went down, so we never did get to finish our conversation. And I never saw the guy again after that. I guess he didn't make it. So, I still don't know how to answer that question. I haven't been inside a church, now, in years. Not since Helen died."

They pulled into Wilhelmina's driveway. She fumbled for something to say. "Would you like to come in for a while? I can make some coffee . . ."

"Well, it's late. I don't want to keep you up past your bedtime."

Wilhelmina had never entertained a man all alone in her life. Her brothers would be horrified. But she looked at Mike's thin, pale face and saw that time was running out.

"Please, Mike. I'd like to hear the end of your story."

"What story's that?"

"About your plane being shot down."

He looked at her curiously, "Are you insisting?"

"Yes. I'm insisting. Come on."

He turned off the truck and followed her through the front door. She heard him whistle softly as he walked into her elegant living room.

"Quite a place. Lori told me it was like a mansion."

"Don't be silly. Sit down, please, and make yourself at home. I'll put some coffee on."

When she returned a few minutes later Mike was standing in front of the fireplace, admiring the trophy she had won in the kite contest.

"Where're all the others?" he asked.

"The others . . . ?"

"Yeah, the trophies you won for playing the piano?"

"Heavens! That was ages ago. I haven't kept all those silly things around."

"You're too modest. If you win something, you should be proud. Brag it up a little bit."

Wilhelmina's hands shook as she set the cups on the coffee table. How was she going to draw the conversation back to religion?

"I meant it when I said I'd like to hear the rest of your story," she began.

"OK, but it'll cost you. If I tell you a story, you'll

have to play me a song. Fair enough?"

"Do you have a request?"

"Whatever you want," he said, laughing. "I don't care. Hey, maybe you can play that ballet thing you took Lori to see."

"That was a two-hour performance!"

"Whatever. Play just a little of it, then."

"All right, if that's your request. Now, you were flying a dangerous mission over Germany after discussing religion with another pilot, when . . ."

Mike smiled and sat down beside her on the sofa. He took a few sips of his coffee, then leaned back comfortably.

"I never did know exactly what hit me. There was a huge explosion. *Bang!* And the whole tail section was gone. Smoke and flames everywhere. I tried to keep the nose up so maybe I could gain more time and ditch it out over the ocean, but it was hopeless. So I decided I'd better bail out. It was the first time I ever jumped at night. The last time, too, come to think of it. It was pitch black except for some artillery fire way off on the horizon somewhere. No moon, no stars, and I couldn't tell how close I was to the ground until I hit it."

"Were you in Germany?"

"Occupied France. Same difference, almost. Nazis everywhere. I heard some of them firing at me as I parachuted down. Felt like a duck in a shooting gallery. Good thing it was so dark, or they might have hit me.

"I landed pretty hard in the middle of a field, and I

212

thought for sure I'd broken both ankles. They were just bruised, though. My first thought was to get as far away from the chute as possible and take cover. So I untangled myself and crawled along the ground to a clump of bushes on the edge of the field. All the time I was waiting for the Nazis to start using me for target practice again.

"By now every farm dog in France was barking up a storm, so I figured I'd better keep moving. I followed the fence line as far as I could because there was tall grass and bushes growing all along it for cover. It was early springtime and there was a light dusting of snow on the ground, and I remember thinking I was probably leaving a trail that any schoolkid could follow, but I didn't know what else to do. I was cold too. Damp and cold.

"Before too long I saw flashlights coming across the field, heading toward the place where I'd left the chute. Looked like four or five of them."

"Nazis?"

"I didn't know, but I wasn't gonna stick around and find out. I started to run, ducking down and hobbling along on two sore ankles, and all the while looking back over my shoulder at them, and thanking God that there was no moon. Sure enough, they found the chute, then started following the trail I'd made for them in the snow."

"What did you do?"

"I ran faster! All of a sudden, *wham!* I went down with a crash and oh, boy, did I see stars!"

"They *shot* you?"

"Nope, I tripped over a fence wire, strung about a foot off the ground. I'd been running so fast I never even saw it, and I hit the frozen ground so hard I knocked myself clean out.

"I came to a few minutes later, I guess, because they were all standing over me. No uniforms, just farmer-type clothes, and they were all speaking French, 'boo-sha, boo-sha.' Probably discussing what a bumbling idiot I was. I tried a few English phrases, but they just shook their heads. All they could say was 'America' and point to my uniform. Two of them were carrying my parachute, so I figured they were going to help me hide from the Nazis."

"And did they?"

"Yep. For the next few weeks it was like a game of hide-and-seek and charades all rolled into one. Only it wasn't a game. They hid me in cellars and closets and hay barns and woodpiles. I never stayed in any one place too long. The French underground kept moving me, little by little, all over France it seemed. Sometimes they'd dress me like a peasant, sometimes like your grandmother, and I think they even had a Nazi uniform on me at one point.

"All the time, I didn't understand a word of their 'boo-shah boo-shah' or have a clue where I was going or who I was with. I just had to trust them, see? Whether I understood them or not, because there was no way I could help myself. I just did whatever they wanted me to, dressed however they said, went wherever they led me, and eventually I wound up back in England, safe and sound."

"How long did it take?"

"Oh, somewhere between three and four weeks, I think. I ended up on a dinky fishing boat crossing the English Channel with two other pilots, a British fellow and a Canadian. I'll tell you, being out in the water in that flimsy little boat in the dead of night sure made me glad I didn't join the navy!"

"Did they send you home after your terrible ordeal?"

"What for? I wasn't injured or anything. I apologized for wrecking their beautiful P-51 and they gave me another one to fly, just like it."

"And you had to fly back there again?"

"Sure, why not? No reason to stay on the ground. Boy, those were beautiful planes. Flew like a Cadillac." He sat lost in thought for a moment. Wilhelmina saw another opening.

"Well, you certainly must have thanked God for saving you."

"Yep, and I had a few words of thanks for the French underground too. Hey! You owe me a song now, remember?"

"Yes, I remember. You wanted 'Romeo and Juliet,' but I don't think I have any music for that. Or if I do, I wouldn't know where to find it."

"It doesn't matter. Play anything you want. You could lie and tell me it's that ballet thing. How would I know?"

Wilhelmina was smiling as she sat down at the bench. She gazed back at Mike, slouched contentedly on her sofa with his legs outstretched, his hands locked comfortably behind his head. *Do you love him?* her friend Catherine had asked. Her words were useless without love.

Mike. He was so kind and gentle, almost tender at times, and suddenly Wilhelmina knew it wasn't merely a sense of duty that made her want to share Christ with him. He had touched her heart, shared a part of his fleeting life with her, and she longed to share everlasting life with him in return.

"How about 'Moonlight Sonata' by Beethoven?"

Mike smiled. "Sure."

Mike watched in fascination as Wilhelmina got ready to play. She sat very still at the keyboard for a moment, with her head down, as if concentrating on the music. He wondered if that was like all the pre-flight checks he had to make each time he flew. Then she arched her long, elegant hands and began to play, a slow, haunting melody, poignantly sad, yet delicately beautiful. After a few minutes, Mike recognized it. It was the same song he had heard through the walls of Dr. Bennett's office the day he learned he was going to die. He swallowed the lump in his throat as the memory returned. He wanted her to stop. He didn't want to think about dying on his last night of life.

But Wilhelmina was so involved in the music,

playing with such depth of emotion and feeling, that it seemed wrong to disturb her. He watched her hands as she lovingly caressed the keys, like a mother caressing her newborn. They were strong, youthful hands. He saw tiny beads of sweat form on her forehead. All of the energy and vigor that he poured into living his life to the fullest, she had invested in her music. All her strength, all her emotion, all her passion. And the result was this moving, rapturous sound.

No wonder she was so deeply depressed since her retirement. It wasn't fun and adventure that she lacked. They had taken away her only means of expression—her life and her soul. He tried to imagine never flying again, never feeling the thrill of liftoff, the freedom to soar the skies. He swallowed hard.

The piece only lasted a few minutes, but by the time she finished playing the final, melancholy note it was as if she'd been transported someplace else. He didn't disturb the silence that followed until she finally relaxed and turned to him. Then he applauded softly.

"That was beautiful," he whispered. Their eyes met, and for a moment a wordless recognition of the peculiar sort of love they shared passed between them. Then Mike looked away, suddenly afraid that she'd also recognize his unspoken farewell. He stood and walked over to the piano. "Do you have an encore? Maybe something with a few loops and dives and barrel rolls in it?"

She gave him a puzzled look. "You mean *arpeggios?*"

He laughed. "I don't know what I mean. It's like we speak two different languages, flying lingo and music lingo."

"Is this what you want?" Her fingers flew up and down the keyboard at an awesome speed yet found each note with the precision of a surgeon. She stopped abruptly, after about a minute.

"Oh, don't stop! That was incredible! Like watching an air show or something."

Wilhelmina laughed out loud. "My playing has been called a lot of things by the critics, but that's the first time I've ever been compared to an air show. I'm flattered—I think."

"I meant it as a compliment. What was that song? Play the rest."

"That was the third movement of the same piece, the 'Moonlight Sonata.' But I don't remember the rest very well without the music."

"You know, I think I could grow to like your kind of music if I kept listening to it. What's your favorite song?"

"Goodness! There are thousands of works. How can I pick just one?"

"I don't know, I've flown a lot of aircraft through the years, but I still think I could pick a favorite if I had to."

"Well, if I limited it to the piano repertory . . ." She seemed lost in thought for a moment. "I guess I would have to say 'The Emperor Concerto' by Beethoven."

"Can you play me some of it?"

"Well, it's a concerto, you see. I'd need an orchestra. But I have a recording of it, if you'd like to hear that?"

"Is it a recording of you?"

"I'm afraid not."

"Too bad. Oh well, sure. Play it anyway."

She put the record on the stereo, and Mike listened to the loud, majestic opening. He smiled appreciatively. "I like that. Who did you say wrote it?"

"Ludwig van Beethoven."

"Well then, Beethoven sounds like a man who really enjoyed life. Listen to that . . . full of joy and fun."

"Actually, he didn't have a very easy life, Mike. He lost his hearing—one of the most horrible tragedies that a musician could ever face. By the time he died he was almost stone deaf."

"So he had to stop writing music?"

"No, he continued to compose, but he probably never heard his own music the way we hear it. Only in his mind. He was partially deaf when he composed this concerto."

"Well, that explains why this song is bursting with life."

"What do you mean?"

"Beethoven was dealt a really hard blow, right? But instead of letting it get him down, he poured his heart and soul into his music and created something truly beautiful instead."

He saw tears well up in her eyes. He'd better change the subject, fast.

"Hey, will you listen to that? It sounds like two pianos playing at once."

"No, it's only one."

"Does the guy have three hands, then? How can he play two songs at once like that?" She didn't answer. "What did you say this was called? A concerto?"

"Yes. It's like a contest between the orchestra and a solo instrument, in this case, the piano."

"That's just what it sounds like too. First one team goes at it, then the other. What instrument is that, playing right now?"

"That's an oboe."

Mike pinched the end of his nose. "Sounds like a duck with a cold. What's that one?"

"French horn."

They sat down on the sofa again, and she explained the music to him as the concerto played. She used fancy words like *motif* and *exposition, development,* and *recapitulation,* until she was talking way over his head. But she seemed so engrossed in her lecture, so happy to be teaching again, that he didn't have the heart to tell her he was lost. As the first movement neared the end, they both fell silent, listening. The delicate, tinkling melody nearly brought tears to his eyes. He thought of his wife. Helen loved pretty things.

"That was beautiful," Mike whispered. "Like a music box."

"Do you want to hear the rest?" He nodded and she rose to turn over the record. As the first few bars of the waltz-like melody played, Mike stood up and bowed.

"May I have this dance, my lady? Or is it sacrilegious to waltz to Beethoven?"

"Well . . . uh . . . I don't know."

"Listen, anyone who loved life as much as Beethoven did, wouldn't mind if we danced to his music. Come on." He took her in his arms before she could protest and waltzed grandly around the room with her. At first her body felt stiff and resisting in his arms, but as the power and beauty of the stately melody took over, she soon relaxed. In the comfort of her embrace, Mike felt some of his sorrow and heaviness begin to lift. He held her close. She smelled good, like lavender and Ivory soap.

As they waltzed past the mirror above the mantelpiece, Mike saw what a comical pair they made. Wilhelmina was at least five or six inches taller than he was. But as he swung her around, he also saw that her eyes were closed and that tears were falling silently down her cheeks. He hoped he hadn't said something wrong. But maybe she needed to hold someone in her arms as much as he did. They clung to each other, dancing to the entire second movement in silence.

Toward the end, the music slowed nearly to a stop. Then, after a few tentative notes, the final movement suddenly took off at a rollicking pace. Mike swung into the new tempo and they galloped around the room together, bumping into furniture and nearly knocking over two lamps and an end table. Finally, they were both laughing so hard they had to collapse on the sofa.

"I'll bet ol' Mr. Beethoven had a good time composing that!" Mike said when he caught his breath again.

"I suppose you see him sitting at his music desk, laughing heartily while he wrote?"

"He never wrote this sitting at any desk! Listen to it! He was outside somewhere. Under a tree, maybe."

"You're right, you know. That's what all the books say. He composed outdoors—or at least got his inspiration there. I don't know why, but I always pictured him at a desk. Serious. Somber. Dignified."

"No way! Just listen to that music. He was having fun."

As the concerto neared the end, the music slowed, gradually growing softer until it almost died quietly away. Then it took off again, ending with a majestic finale.

"Boy, for a minute, there, I thought it was gonna die a quiet death," Mike said. "But see? Ol' Beethoven decided to end it all with a whoop and a bang after all."

Wilhelmina's expression suddenly changed. "Mike, we need to talk," she said shakily.

"Sure, what about?"

"You've had several months to reconsider and I . . . I was hoping that you've changed your mind about

". . . uh . . . ending your own life."

Mike passed his hand over his face. His approaching death wasn't something he wanted to talk about. It was something he just had to do. He stood up.

"It's late. I should be going."

"Mike, no! Please! Can't we at least talk about it?"

"No. No, we can't. You have no idea how hard it is for me to do this, but I have to. I was hoping you'd forgotten all about it by now. I never really meant to tell you in the first place." He took a few steps toward the door.

"Oh, Mike, please listen to me. It's not God's will for you to commit suicide. The Bible says—"

"Wilhelmina, don't." He turned his back on her and walked the rest of the way to the door. She followed.

"Mike, please don't leave here angry with me."

He turned to her. "I'm not mad at you, Willymina. But, don't you see? I can't let you talk me out of it. I can't. I'm sorry." He gently took her hand and pressed it to his cheek. "Thank you for a very memorable evening," he whispered. "Good night."

As soon as the door closed, Wilhelmina let out an anguished cry. She had run out of time. She would probably never see Mike again.

All of the missed opportunities and unspoken words came flooding back to her in a deluge. Why hadn't she tried harder to talk to him? Mike was dying without knowing Christ, and she had been too wrapped up in her own misery to meet his needs.

Couldn't she have forgotten her own problems for a few hours for his sake? She had been angry with God, but she had punished Mike for it. She stared in agony at her closed front door. *"Here I am! I stand at the door and knock."*

"O God, forgive me," she wept.

She wandered into the living room and saw how disheveled it looked. The oriental carpets were bunched and wrinkled. Lamp shades and furniture were knocked askew. One of her African violets was upside down on the floor. Even the oil paintings seemed to hang crookedly on the walls. The usually impeccable room had been disarranged by their wild, galloping dance.

That's what meeting Mike had done to her life. He had turned her orderly, predictable life upside down. As she gazed at her mantelpiece where the gaudy kite trophy had upstaged her grandmother's antique clock, Wilhelmina thought of a question she hadn't bothered to ask before: Why had Mike gone out of his way to include her in his life?

Why had he taken her to the kite contest? Or fishing? Why had he invited her to go to the balloon race tonight? She had stayed in contact with him in order to witness to him, but why had he bothered with a sour old stuffed shirt like her? Why had he worked so hard to cheer her up, treating her with tenderness and compassion?

Mike's life had demonstrated more of the love of Christ than hers had. Mike heard music in the rustling leaves. *The leaves actually sacrifice themselves,* he'd told her. *They fall off the branches and die, just so the tree can survive.* Mike perceived the peace of God in the quiet forest. He recognized hope in Beethoven's music where there should have been despair. She saw now that there had been dozens of opportunities to share the gospel message with him, but she'd been too consumed with self-pity to notice them.

Wilhelmina sank down on the sofa as memories of Mike washed gently over her. She saw him shaking her hand after the piano recital and, with a grin, firmly closing the lid on that awful piano. He had been right, of course. It was out of tune. But like the child in "The Emperor's New Clothes," he was the only one who had been honest enough to say it.

She remembered the day in the doughnut shop when he sprang from his seat and grabbed her by the hand, ready that instant to take her flying with him. She saw him at the kite contest, sprinting across the grass with his keys jangling in his pocket, his round face and crinkly smile turned up to the sky, encouraging her and his grandchildren to try again. She recalled his silly conversation with a tree in the state park and all his efforts to cheer her up that day when he could have simply taken her home. She thought of how he'd arranged for her to ride in Max's hot air balloon, yet he didn't get angry when she'd refused. And she remembered the warmth of his gentle touch and the stubble of his cheek as he'd held her in his arms

tonight and waltzed with her to the "Emperor Concerto."

In all of her memories, Mike was smiling and
waving his silly baseball cap. But she was always
frowning. Which one of them had been witnessing?

"What on earth is the matter with me?" she cried
aloud. "How could I have been so selfish?"

If only she could go back and start all over again. If
only she had another chance. But she knew from the
way he had said "good night" that it was really "good-
bye."

Wilhelmina dropped to her knees beside the sofa
and buried her head in the sofa cushions where Mike
had sat. Prayer had always been little more than a
ritual to her, performed out of a sense of duty or sometimes a need. Now, for the first time in her life, she
cried out to God with all her passion and strength.
Time had run out for Mike. Prayer was the only option
left.

13

Sunday, October 25, 1987

By the time Mike got home, it was 1:30 in the
morning. Buster and Heinz greeted him with sleepy
enthusiasm, then curled up on the bearskin rug and
went back to sleep. Mike regretted running out on
Wilhelmina, but he knew how vulnerable he had felt.

He couldn't take a chance that she would talk him out of his decision. He stood in the middle of his cluttered living room, engulfed by overwhelming sorrow. In a few more hours his life would be over.

He gazed at Helen's picture on the piano through his tears. He had thought about Helen so much these past few days, remembering how she had lain in bed for so long, her life painfully ebbing away. She must have felt the same way he did right now, aware that she was going to die but wishing that she could live.

Mike had faced death several times before in his life—when he was shot down over France, when his engine failed over the Adirondacks, when he faced his first cancer surgery. Each time had been terrifying because he hadn't been sure what the outcome would be. But this time he knew the outcome with certainty, just as Helen had known. Yet she had faced death courageously, without self-pity. He wished she were here to strengthen him.

He wandered into their bedroom and sat down on the edge of the bed, her side of the bed. He stared at the floor. She had been gone for more than 17 years, yet tonight the ache in his heart was as great as on the day she had died. He needed her. But there was no way to bring her back.

He sat in the dark, motionless, for a long time until the need to hold her, to touch even a small part of her, overwhelmed him. He switched on the lamp and opened the small drawer in her bedside stand, searching for something that had once been hers.

He cried out when he saw it. Helen's Bible felt limp in his hands as he tenderly lifted it out. Its spine was long broken, its pages thin and ragged from use. He held it to his chest, remembering how much she had treasured it, what an important part of her life it had once been. He closed his eyes and saw her again, sitting at the kitchen table reading it, tucking it under her arm as she left with the boys for church every Sunday, placing it in the drawer after reading it every night.

He whispered her name as he fingered the words, *Helen Ann Dolan*, embossed in gold on the cover. This tired, worn book with the pages falling out had been Helen's strength, her consolation. He opened it, wishing he could draw courage from it, too, and saw that she had underlined many verses. Tucked inside it were dozens of small notes and keepsakes. As he thumbed through it, it seemed to Mike that she sat beside him, guiding him through the well-worn pages, marked with reminders of her life and the people she loved.

First it fell open to a faded black and white photograph of Mike Jr. and Steve, wearing plaid flannel pajamas, seated in front of a scrawny Christmas tree. Their new puppy, Queenie, was wriggling out of Steve's arms. Little Mike wore a broad grin, proudly showing that his two front teeth were missing. Mike smiled, too, remembering the popular song that year, "All I Want for Christmas Is My Two Front Teeth." Helen's writing on the back of the photo gave their ages. *Michael Jr., age 6. Steven, age 4, with Queenie.*

Sweet, happy memories filled Mike's heart. All those Christmases so many years ago. Toy trucks and, of course, toy airplanes. Assembling stubborn bicycle parts at midnight on Christmas Eve. Helen's hand-knit mittens and stocking caps. The joy and delight on the boys' faces on Christmas morning. Lean years and good years. A lifetime of memories from a simple photograph.

His eye was drawn to a verse on the same page. Helen had underlined it in red. *"Sons are a heritage from the LORD, children a reward from him."*

Mike returned the photograph to its place and flipped ahead until the Bible fell open again, near the end. An old photograph of himself, taken during the war, marked this spot. He was in uniform, and his hand rested on the fuselage of his P-51 Mustang.

"Best aircraft I ever flew," he murmured. Helen had chosen his favorite picture. But that was the way Helen was—never demanding her own way, always giving her family the things that would make them happy.

For some crazy reason, Mike thought of stuffed peppers. They were Helen's favorite, and she always ordered them whenever he took her out to the City Diner. Yet in all their years of marriage she never once cooked them for dinner because Mike couldn't stand them. It seemed to him now that throughout their years together, Helen had always given unselfishly. And he had always taken.

Like going to church. It had meant so much to her. Why hadn't he gone with her once in awhile, at least at Christmas or Easter? He could have done one unselfish thing to make her happy, but she'd never asked for anything for herself. And he had never offered. There had always been another engine to repair, another charter to fly.

He noticed that a verse on this page was also underlined in red and he blinked back his tears as he read it. *"Wives, in the same way be submissive to your husbands so that, if any of them do not believe the word, they may be won over without words by the behavior of their wives, when they see the purity and reverence of your lives."*

He closed the Bible and wiped the tears off as they dropped, one by one, onto the faded cover. It was painful to read this Book, her book. It revealed a familiar world to him but from Helen's point of view, as if he were inside her heart, seeing it through her eyes. He'd discovered a part of her he had never bothered to notice before.

But like a blind man longing for the light, in the end Mike longed to see more than he feared the pain of being shown. He wiped his tears and reopened the Book.

A scrap of yellow, lined notebook paper caught his eye, the writing on it a chunky, irregular scrawl that probably belonged to one of his sons. He unfolded the page and Mike Jr.'s graduation picture fell out. The page must have been part of a longer letter, for it had no real beginning or ending but was numbered at the top, "page 3":

". . . so all we can do is keep the choppers flying back and forth with spit and prayers.

"You get to thinking a lot about life and death over here, maybe because you see so much of it all around you every day. When you're back home in church the Bible and all that stuff can seem like a lot of fairy tales and even though you always dragged Steve and me to Sunday School every week, inside I always felt kind of proud that I didn't need religion for a crutch. But over here in Nam your best buddy can be alive one minute, laughing and joking around, and the next minute he's blown in a hundred pieces and it makes you think, what's it all about anyway?

"The night after my buddy Rick was killed I was hurting so bad I didn't know what else to do, so I got out the Bible you sent me. And all those stories I had heard all my life about Jesus dying on the Cross, all of a sudden didn't seem like fairy tales any more because I have seen death, and now I know what His death really meant. I've seen mankind (and myself) at our very worst over here, and at last I understand why Jesus had to die for me. It's like all the pieces fell into place. I'm glad I'm not on bombing missions like Rick was or dropping napalm, because I can't hate the Vietcong anymore. I don't know where it all went, but my hatred is gone since I accepted Christ.

We'll talk more when I come home.

"Did Queenie have her pups, yet? Don't forget, I promised one to Kathy's brother, so make sure he gets first pick . . ."

A shiver passed through Mike as he stared at his son's picture. He remembered what Mike Jr.'s commanding officer had told them about his last flight. He was on a volunteer mission over enemy territory, picking up wounded Vietnamese civilians when he was shot down.

Mike looked down at the Book to see what passage Helen had underlined to mark this very painful chapter in their life. He read the words, *"For God so loved the world that he gave his one and only Son, that whoever believes in him shall not perish but have eternal life."*

Mike remembered those terrible months that followed Mike Jr.'s funeral. He had been so lost in his own grief and guilt that he had pushed aside all of Helen's efforts to console him. He had blamed himself for his son's death. If he hadn't glorified his own war exploits . . . if he hadn't pushed his son into flying . . . Mike Jr. had sat on his lap in the cockpit and held the controls of a plane almost before he could walk.

But even though Mike had blamed himself, Helen never had. He could only guess at the pain she must have silently suffered at losing her son, but he had been unable to offer her comfort or consolation. This scrap of a letter, this verse in the Bible must have been what sustained her, what had soothed her grief and given her hope.

Mike had opened Helen's Bible to see and touch a part of her. Instead he was seeing himself, and the picture was devastating. Even so, he couldn't turn back until the portrait was complete.

He found another marked spot and another picture. It was Steve, taken just before he left for Vietnam. He was in his marine uniform. Unsmiling. Hair shorn. Jaw set in angry determination to avenge his brother's death. His heart filled with hatred and rage. Mike remembered how hard Helen had cried the day Steve shipped out. At the time he'd thought it was from fear of losing Steve too. But now he wondered if there was another reason.

After Mike Jr.'s funeral Steve had refused to attend church with his mother. "There is no God!" he had screamed at her. "How could a loving God let this happen?"

When Helen had tried to talk to Steve, Mike had interfered. "Leave him alone! You and your religion! How can you still believe God answers your prayers?"

Steve had never gone to church again. He had abandoned all his friends from church and found new ones to smoke pot with and drink beer. Whenever Helen had tried to talk to him, Mike had always taken Steve's side.

Mike looked down for the underlined verse. What had been her prayer for Steven? *"Train a child in the way he should go, and when he is old he will not depart from it.*"

Mike flipped slowly through the Bible, skipping hundreds of underlined verses. He stopped when he found another folded piece of paper. It was part of a church bulletin. It was dated two weeks before Helen died. Along with the usual church announcements there was a poem:

*He giveth more grace when the burdens grow
    greater;*
*He sendeth more strength when the labors
    increase.*
To added affliction He addeth His mercy;
To multiplied trials, His multiplied peace.

His love has no limit; His grace has no measure.
His pow'r has no boundary known unto men.
For out of His infinite riches in Jesus,
He giveth, and giveth, and giveth again!

Mike had taken care of his wife throughout her long illness. But God had been the Source of her inner strength and courage. He had rewarded her faith with His abiding peace. In spite of all her suffering, Helen's last words had been "Lord Jesus," her last gift to Mike, a smile.

She had underlined a long passage beside this poem, but Mike read it all, hungry to experience Helen's peace.

"I consider that our present sufferings are not worth comparing with the glory that will be revealed in us . . . and we know that in all things God works for the good of those who love him . . . He who did not spare his own Son, but gave him up for us all—how will he not also, along with him, graciously give us all things? . . . Who shall separate us from the love of Christ? . . . I am convinced that neither death nor life . . . nor anything else in all creation, will be able to separate us from the love of God that is in Christ Jesus our Lord."

If only he could ask her what it meant. Helen had shared his life, shared his hopes and dreams, his love of airplanes and flying. But he had never asked her about her faith. Why hadn't he acted differently, been more sensitive, more caring? He saw the selfish way he'd lived his life, and he hated what he saw.

Mike closed the Book. Tears of regret, sorrow, and guilt washed down his face. He sat, unmoving, for a long time, holding Helen's Bible in his arms as if he held her.

At last he wiped his eyes and opened it again. He wanted to read it. All of it. He wanted to find what Helen had found. He paged impatiently past the title page and table contents until he came to the first chapter of Genesis. A small white envelope, unnoticed before, slid from the Book and drifted to the floor. He bent to pick it up and recognized Helen's writing—*"To Mike."* The envelope was sealed.

He opened it with shaking fingers and pulled out a letter, dated the week of her death.

"My Beloved Mike,

"How I have prayed for the day when you would open the pages of this Bible, the most precious of all books. I can only guess why you've opened it now. To search for answers? To find comfort? Or hope? Whatever the reason, I know you will find what you're searching for because I have tested it and found God's Word to be more than sufficient for all of my needs. Even now, as I face death, His Word sustains me and gives me peace.

"I love you, Mike. Yet in the depths of that love I find my deepest regret—I have never found a way to share my faith in Christ with you. God knows how hard I've tried, how I've prayed for a chance to tell you what my faith means to me. But I have never found a way.

"You're such a good man, such a wonderful father and husband. You provide so unselfishly for all our needs. How can I show you your need of a Savior? You've never run after other women, you don't have a violent temper—how can I tell you that you have sinned or fallen short of the glory of God? You are the kindest, gentlest, most loving man I've ever known.

"I have turned to God because I saw the sin in my heart and I knew I needed to be changed. I drew strength from God because I was weak. But you have always been so capable, so strong, so independent.

Please forgive me, but I never knew how to tell you that you need to put your life in God's hands and let Him take control of it.

"Remember when the boys were little and they wanted to fly an airplane so badly? You would put them in the pilot's seat and let them hold the stick and they always thought they were in control, that they were really flying the plane. But you were holding the dual controls in your hand all the time, keeping the plane in the air, landing it safely again. What a disaster it would have been If they had really tried to fly alone!

"God has been with you all your life, Mike, guiding you, keeping you on course, even though you always thought you were running your own life. He loves you, just as you love your sons. More than anything else He wants to see you land safely in His kingdom.

"I pray for you and for Steven every day of the life that is left to me. I pray as Jesus once prayed, 'Father, I want those you have given me to be with me where I am.' I have faith that Michael is already waiting in heaven for me, but how can it truly be paradise if you and Steven aren't there with us?

"I know that God hears my prayers, and I have to trust that somehow, someday, He will send someone into your life who will lead you to kneel before the cross of Christ. I have to trust and believe that when the day comes that you also face death, as I now do, you will know and understand those words of Jesus: 'I am the resurrection and the life. He who believes in

*me will live, even though he dies; and whoever lives
and believes in me will never die.'*

"The Book in your hands holds the answers to all
the questions you could ever ask. Mike, put your hand
in God's and let Him lead you.

"I love you with all my heart,

"Helen."

• • •

The knock on Wilhelmina's door was so soft that at
first she thought she had imagined it. But after her
grandmother's clock finished striking 3 A.M., she
heard it again. She rose from her knees and hurried to
the door. Mike stood on her front step, clutching a tattered Bible.

"I . . . uh . . . saw your lights on . . . and . . . I—"

Wilhelmina enfolded him in her arms and held him
close. He clung to her.

Thank You, God. Thank You.

At last she led him into the living room and sat
beside him on the sofa. She waited for him to speak
first.

"I needed to talk to someone . . . I . . ." He took a
deep, shuddering breath and let it out slowly. "All my
life I've been in the pilot's seat, making my own flight
plans, handling all the controls . . . Then tonight, when
I was flying in Max's balloon, I realized that he had a
kind of freedom I never had. He just let go and let the
wind carry him along, and he landed wherever it blew
him. Helen had that kind of freedom . . . that kind of

238

peace. She never tried to control everything herself, like I always did. Am I making any sense?"

"Yes. But do you understand where Helen's peace, Helen's freedom, came from?"

He held up the worn Bible. "Now I do. Now that it's too late. I've made such a mess of my life by trying to run it myself. I've caused a lot of hurt and pain, especially to the people I loved the most. I want to tell God I'm sorry . . . I'm sorry for messing things up . . . but I don't know how. How can I ever make it up to Him, now that my life is almost over?"

"You don't have to, Mike. If you're truly sorry—and I know that you are—then God will forgive you."

His eyes filled with tears. "Just like that?"

"When Jesus died on the Cross, it wasn't for anything He had done. It was for all our mistakes . . . all the things we've done wrong. If you accept His sacrifice as being for you—for your sins—then God will accept it too."

"But why would He do that for me? I've screwed up . . ."

"If you had known that your son was going to die in Vietnam, would you have been willing to trade places with him? To die in his place?"

Mike covered his eyes. "I've wished it had been me instead of Mikey a million times over. He was only 19."

"That's why. God took your place and died for your sins because He loves you. Because you're His child. His love is even greater than the love you have for your children. Jesus died so that you could have eternal life."

"Eternal life . . . but I'm dying."

"When you look at God's amazing love and see the sacrifice He made for you through His Son, can you still believe that He would destroy you forever, at death? God wants to give you life. Everlasting life."

"Is that what this means?"

He gave her a page from a letter. Wilhelmina read the lines he pointed to, aloud. "'I am the resurrection and the life. He who believes in me will live, even though he dies; and whoever lives and believes in me will never die.' Yes, Mike. That's exactly what that means."

"O God, forgive me!" he wept.

"Let's talk to Him . . . together." She knelt in front of the sofa, and Mike knelt beside her, covering his face with his hands. They prayed together, weeping tears of repentance, tears of joy.

14

When the sun rose that morning, Mike was sitting at Wilhelmina's kitchen table, watching her as she scrambled eggs, buttered slices of toast, and fixed a pot of coffee. The silence they shared was warm and full of understanding.

Exhaustion numbed Wilhelmina, making her movements slow and clumsy. But the chorus of praise that she sang in her heart lifted her above her fatigue. The coffeepot swam in front of her as she blinked back her happy tears. She had just set the food on the table when the telephone rang.

"Hi, it's Carol. I need a ride to church this morning. Can you pick me up?"

Was it Sunday? Wilhelmina had completely forgotten what day it was. She glanced at the kitchen clock and realized she would have to hurry.

"Sure, Carol. I'll be there in about half an hour."

"Your voice sounds hoarse. Don't you feel well, dear?"

"I'm fine, just tired. I'll see you in a little while."

Mike was studying his watch. "I'd better be going. You've got plans."

"My friend Carol needs a ride to church. And I'm scheduled to play the organ." She watched him push his scrambled eggs around on his plate. "Mike . . . would you like to come with us?"

"I would . . . but . . . uh . . . I've got a flight scheduled this morning."

"Another time, maybe?"

He didn't look up. "Yeah, sure. Another time."

Mike seemed unusually quiet as Wilhelmina quickly finished her breakfast. He ate very little. The silence between them felt awkward now, and she wished she didn't have to rush off and leave him so abruptly. She was about to apologize for her haste, when Mike looked at his watch again, then quickly stood up.

"Gosh, it's late. I'd better take off. Steve will be

wondering what happened to me."

Wilhelmina followed him to the door, struggling to find the right words to say. But before she could speak, Mike suddenly gathered her in his arms and held her tightly.

"Thanks. For everything," he whispered. Then he was gone.

Wilhelmina dried her eyes and hurried upstairs to change for church. When she remembered the TV and newspaper coverage of the balloon race, she groaned. If only she could stay home today. She gazed at her reflection in the mirror in dismay. Dark circles ringed her eyes. They were still red and puffy from crying. Her hair was a fright, but there was no time to fix it properly. Carol was certain to comment on how awful she looked. But Wilhelmina couldn't explain to her the beauty of what happened last night. Nor the strange mixture of joy and sadness she now felt. Perhaps someday she would be able to share the miracle that she had witnessed and that God had allowed her to be a part of but certainly not today. If she couldn't even think about Mike without tears springing to her eyes, how could she possibly talk about what God had done in his life?

By the time Wilhelmina arrived at Carol's house, she was later than she'd promised. Carol looked offended. She was lugging two plastic grocery bags filled with grape juice and saltine crackers, and she struggled to get into the car with them.

"Honestly, Wilhelmina. You know I'm supposed to

be there early today. This is the last Sunday of the month, remember? That means it's Communion Sunday and I have to—"

"The last day of the month?" Inside Wilhelmina's weary mind something suddenly clicked. She jammed on the brakes, sending Carol's grocery bags flying off the seat onto the floor.

"Good heavens! What is the matter with you? You almost broke the juice bottles!"

Wilhelmina remembered the letter from the aviation medical examiner on the dashboard of Mike's truck. Peter had read it to her, slowly sounding out each word. She recalled how quiet Mike had been at breakfast, how hurriedly he had left, and Wilhelmina suddenly realized the truth. Mike's medical certificate expired today. He was on his way to fly his last flight.

"*O dear God!* Carol, get out! Get out of the car!"

"Wilhelmina! What on earth—!"

"Don't ask questions. There's no time. Just get out!"

Carol groped for the door handle, her eyes wide with fright. "What is the matter with you?"

"I can't go to church this morning. Tell Pastor Stockman I won't be there."

"But . . . what about the organ and—?"

"Carol, *please!* I've got to hurry!"

"But . . . but . . . how will I get to church?"

Wilhelmina shoved her purse into Carol's hands. "Here. There's money in my wallet. Take a cab. Now please, get out of the car!"

Carol quickly gathered her parcels and opened the door. She stared at Wilhelmina in bewilderment as she stepped onto the sidewalk. "I don't know what on earth has gotten into you lately, but—"

Wilhelmina never heard the rest. As soon as the car door slammed, she made a U-turn in the middle of the street, tires squealing, and left Carol standing beside the road with two grocery bags and Wilhelmina's purse piled high in her arms. Then she drove as fast as she could across town, pleading with God to get her there in time.

The area around the airport was a maze of access roads and hangars. She had no idea where to find Dolan Aviation. Wilhelmina drove wildly, trying to keep one eye on the road, the other on the dozens of signs that seemed to point her in every direction at once. She steered down one dead-end road after another until she was frantic. With little activity at the airport on a Sunday morning, no one was around to give her directions.

As she paused at an intersection, trying to decide which way to turn, she suddenly heard the roar of an airplane. A small, single-engine propeller plane sat on the taxiway at the far end of the road. *Dear God, please let it be Mike!*

Wilhelmina pressed her foot to the floor and sped down the road as fast as her car would go. When she got to the end, she could read the dark blue lettering on the side of the plane: *Dolan Aviation*. But a tall, chain-link fence separated the road from the taxiway.

She turned right and raced down the access road that ran parallel to the fence, searching for a gate. When she finally found one, she steered through it and drove full speed across the tarmac.

Mike was tinkering with something underneath the plane by the landing gear. He looked up in surprise as the car screeched to a stop and Wilhelmina jumped out. Her chest hurt from her pounding heart. What should she say to him? How should she begin? She told herself to slow down. She had to act calm, not panicked. She couldn't scare him away again.

"Aren't you supposed to be in church?" Mike asked.

"You promised me a ride, remember?" She had to shout to be heard above the loud drone of the engine. "I've decided to go flying with you today, instead."

Mike stared at her for a long moment, then shook his head. "Not this time, Willymina."

She could barely hear him. She took a few steps closer, her open coat flapping in the wind. "But I'm ready to go now. Please let me come with you."

"I thought you were afraid to fly." He tried to grin, but there was pain in his eyes.

"You're a good pilot. We're not going to crash, are we?"

He looked away, gazing sightlessly across the taxiway toward the distant hills. "Can't you understand? I'm just trying to spare my family a lot of grief and pain."

"But you won't spare them anything. They'll feel the same grief no matter how you die or when."

"Wilhelmina, please stop. Don't make this any harder for me than it already is."

All her life, Wilhelmina had worked to construct a barrier of caution and restraint, hardening it over the years to hold back her true feelings, to keep people at arm's length, to avoid being hurt. But as she looked at Mike, she chose to destroy the wall of indifference. For the first time in her life, she opened her heart.

"Don't you understand, Mike? I love you. I don't want to lose you like this."

"So you'd rather watch me die a little each day, is that it? Hooked up to a bunch of machines as if I wasn't even human anymore? So you and everyone else can stand around and pity me?"

Warm tears flowed down Wilhelmina's cheeks at the thought of Mike slowly wasting away. "You're right," she said at last. "Maybe this really is the best way. But I still want to go with you, Mike."

He stared at her. "Do you know what you're saying?"

"Yes. I know." She took another step closer to him. "All my life I've played it safe, never running the risk of being hurt. Until I met you I never understood what it meant to live. Or to love. But now I do. You've changed my life. And now I don't want to live without you. Please, Mike. Let me die 'living' too."

A passenger jet roared over their heads, drowning

out all other sounds. They stood on the windy tarmac gazing silently at each other. Then the jet was gone, leaving only the sound of the propeller as Mike's plane idled on the taxiway behind them.

At last Mike shook his head. "I can't let you come with me."

"Why not?"

"Because I love you, too, Willymina Brewster. And your life isn't over yet."

"But neither is yours, Mike. Whether it's one week or one month, you've still got the rest of your life to live. You can use whatever time God gives you to talk to your family, to share your new faith with them. Steve still feels bitter toward God. Show him God's love. He'll listen to you. You'd know better than anyone else what to say to him.

"What about Mickey? He wants to be just like you. Teach him what you've learned about trusting in God. And Lori too. She's heard so many conflicting stories about heaven and hell she doesn't know what to believe. But she would believe you. She loves you so much, Mike. And little Peter . . . well, this will break Peter's heart. He thinks you're the greatest pilot in the world. You told me last night that you wanted to stop controlling your own life and let God take over—"

"I do. But I don't understand . . . about death, I mean. I don't understand what God's doing—why my life has to end this way."

"You don't need to understand. Remember when

your plane went down over France? You had to trust your saviors and follow them wherever they led you, whether you understood it or not. If you had tried to find the way yourself, you never would have made it. But you trusted them and you ended up home again, safe and sound. That's the way it is now, Mike. We couldn't understand what God wants to do with our lives even if He explained it to us. We don't speak His language. But we have to trust that whatever He chooses for us is for a good reason and that—"

She stopped short, hearing her own words as if someone was speaking them—to her. "Oh, Mike! I'm talking to myself! God is saying this to me too!"

"What do you mean?"

"I've always been in control of my own life too. I've had it all planned and structured. And I've been mad at God for destroying those plans. When I lost my job at the college, it was as if God told me I had to die. I haven't wanted to submit to His will, either."

Mike wrapped her in his arms and she laid her head on his shoulder. "But if we've really given our lives to Christ," she said, "then our lives should be His, to use in whatever way He chooses."

"So, what you're saying is if I'm going to trust God with my life, then I guess I've got to trust Him even when He asks me to die."

"Yes. And I guess I do too." A small private jet swooped over their heads and landed on the nearby runway. Mike kissed her softly on the cheek, then smiled at her through his tears. A genuine smile, with all the familiar warmth and humor sparkling in his eyes once more.

"Hey, Willymina Brewster. Did I hear you say you came for that plane ride I promised you? Come on. My Cessna's just standing here, all ready to take off."

Wilhelmina's heart began to pound with a new fear. She drew a deep breath. But her life was in God's hands.

"Let's go," she said.

He took her arm and helped her climb into the passenger seat, then ran around to the pilot's side and got in. He gave the engine more throttle, and the little Cessna roared to life. The plane vibrated beneath her. Wilhelmina gripped the seat cushion as they taxied across the tarmac. She looked down the long, open runway and felt her stomach roll over in fear.

"Relax. It'll be smoother than riding in my pickup truck."

"Anything's smoother than your pickup truck!"

The voice of the air traffic controller crackled over the radio. "Roger, Cessna Three-Fox-Charlie, you're cleared for takeoff. And you've got a great day to fly, Mike. Ceiling and visibility unlimited."

Mike smiled at Wilhelmina and gave her a confident "thumbs up." He was at home in this cockpit. She could see how much he loved to fly and how happy it made him to share his joy with her.

He pushed the throttle forward, and the little plane

shot down the runway. Moments later it lifted smoothly off the ground and soared into the clear, blue sky.

EPILOGUE

April 1988

Wilhelmina parked her Buick by the side of the road and turned the engine off. In the backseat, Buster and Heinz began to bark.

"Behave now," she told them. "I'm afraid you have to wait here. I won't be long." She gathered up the bouquet of daffodils and tulips she had picked from her garden that morning and got out of the car.

The early morning air felt cool, but the brilliant spring sun shone warmly on Wilhelmina's back as she walked across the cemetery lawn to Mike's grave. The brown scar of earth stood out against the yellow-green grass all around it. But now that winter was over, new grass would soon grow and by summer his grave would blend in with the ones on either side: Helen's and Mike Jr.'s.

Wilhelmina ran her fingers over Mike's name, etched into the tombstone, as if trying to accept the truth in her heart that he was really gone. *Michael G. Dolan.* Then she knelt and began to place flowers in the bronze pots on each grave.

She was so engrossed in her work, so absorbed with

her memories of Mike, that she didn't hear the approaching footsteps behind her.

"Morning, Miz Brewster."

She gave a little cry and turned to see Mike's friend Max Barker standing behind her. He tipped his hat slightly, then jammed it down on his head once again.

"Sorry, Ma'am. Didn't mean to startle you." He was the same old Max with his stocky build and bulldog scowl, yet this morning he looked different. She couldn't decide why. She rose, brushing the dirt off her knees.

"That's all right, Mr. Barker. I didn't hear you coming, that's all. Where's your truck?"

"I walked over. I only live a couple blocks from here. Get my exercise this way."

The cigar. That's what was missing. Max was no longer chewing on his soggy, unlit cigar. He looked naked without it. He gestured toward her car.

"Are them Mike's dogs?"

"Yes. They came to live with me after . . . now that . . ." She looked down at the ground for a moment, unable to say the words, then back at Max. "They make very fine watchdogs."

He gave an ambiguous grunt and kicked at a stone with the toe of his shoe. "Keepin' busy, Miz Brewster?"

"Me? Why, yes I am. Almost too busy. I've joined the faculty, part-time, at the community college, so I'm traveling there three times a week. And I've got a dozen private piano students that I teach now, including Mike's granddaughter Lori. I've also started a concert series at some area nursing homes, besides all my volunteer work at the Cancer Center . . ."

He grunted again and jammed his hands into his coat pockets. "Guess you're a busy lady."

"How about you, Mr. Barker?"

"Call me Max."

"All right. How have you been, Max?"

He ignored her question. "The reason I asked about you is that . . . well . . ." He shuffled his feet nervously. "Well, the truth is, Mike asked me to kind of keep an eye on you."

She smiled. "That's interesting. He asked me to do the same thing. To keep an eye on you, that is."

"He would." Wilhelmina thought she detected a hint of a smile cross his forbidding features.

She hadn't done what Mike had asked, though. She hadn't even seen Max since Mike's funeral, not knowing how to approach him or what to say. His brusque manner put her off. But here he stood, every bit as uneasy with her as she was with him. Wilhelmina knew what Mike would say. *Life is for living. Take a chance.* If she offered him her friendship, he might reject it. But wasn't Max worth the risk?

"Max . . . I was wondering. I know I didn't do very well the last time, but do you think I could have a second chance? To be on your pit crew, I mean. When you fly your balloon."

252

"Aw, you weren't so bad, Miz Brewster."

"My friends call me Mina."

"At least you found us and picked us up again. I give you some credit for that."

"Then, might I have another chance, Max?"

"Sure." He rubbed his hand over his bristly chin. "Fact is, I entered the New England Balloon Association's annual race. It's held every spring. I could use a good spotter on board."

"You mean in . . . in the balloon?"

"Yeah."

"Oh my! Well, I . . . I suppose I could give that another try."

He grunted again, and this time Wilhelmina was sure it meant he was pleased. "I'll give you a call with all the particulars. Your number in the book?"

She smiled. "Yes. It's in the phone book. Thanks, Max."

He nodded and touched his hat. "Be seeing you."

She watched him stride away, walking with the swaggering gait of a bowlegged sailor. When he disappeared around a bend in the road, she turned back to Mike's grave.

In spite of all the tombstones, it seemed to Wilhelmina that the world around her was bursting with new life. It was in the rich, musky smell of awakening earth. In the tender green buds that dotted the barren branches. In the joyful songs of the robins and chattering squirrels as they raced through the treetops.

She picked up two pebbles, and as she placed one on each tombstone she softly recited the words of Christ:

I am the resurrection and the life.
He who believes in me will live, even
though he dies; and whoever lives and
believes in me will never die.

Center Point Publishing
600 Brooks Road ● PO Box 1
Thorndike ME 04986-0001 USA

(207) 568-3717

US & Canada:
1 800 929-9108